RAZOR'S EDGE
THE HORDE WARS 3

Sherri L. King

RAZOR'S EDGE – *THE HORDE WARS 3*
An Ellora's Cave Publication, December 2004

Ellora's Cave Publishing, Inc.
PO Box 787
Hudson, OH 44236-0787

ISBN #1419950541

Other available formats: MS Reader (LIT), Adobe (PDF),
Rocketbook (RB), Mobipocket (PRC) & HTML

Cover art by *Darrell King*

Warning:

The following material contains graphic sexual content meant for mature readers. *Razor's Edge* has been rated E-rotic by a minimum of three independent reviewers.

Ellora's Cave Publishing offers three levels of Romantica™ reading entertainment: S (S-ensuous), E (E-rotic), and X (X-treme).

S-*ensuous* love scenes are explicit and leave nothing to the imagination.

E-*rotic* love scenes are explicit, leave nothing to the imagination, and are high in volume per the overall word count. In addition, some E-rated titles might contain fantasy material that some readers find objectionable, such as bondage, submission, same sex encounters, forced seductions, etc. E-rated titles are the most graphic titles we carry; it is common, for instance, for an author to use words such as "fucking", "cock", "pussy", etc., within their work of literature.

X-*treme* titles differ from E-rated titles only in plot premise and storyline execution. Unlike E-rated titles, stories designated with the letter X tend to contain controversial subject matter not for the faint of heart.

RAZOR'S EDGE
THE HORDE WARS 3

As always,
For D.

Lead me from the unreal to the real!
Lead me from darkness to light!
Lead me from death to immortality!
-The Upanishads (800-500 B.C.)

Who ever loved that loved not at first sight?
-William Shakespeare

Prologue

"Freeze, asshole!"

The giant in the black trench coat did as she commanded and slowly raised his hands in a gesture of surrender. As he did so, Emily carefully advanced on him, her Glock 23 service handgun aimed and at the ready should the man prove threatening.

"Just what do you think you're doing, here, huh?" With one hand she retrieved her handcuffs and moved behind him. "Hands behind your head," she bit out. "Running around with knives is dangerous—didn't your mother ever tell you that?"

The man didn't acknowledge her, except to follow her order and slowly place his hands behind his head. Emily huffed and wondered idly where her backup was. She'd called in her position several minutes ago while she'd still been in hot pursuit of the man in the black coat. Not that the man had seemed to notice her pursuit. He'd been too busy throwing his knives at some ruffian gang members who'd at least been wise enough to her presence that they'd kept themselves concealed in shadow.

"Why'd you run? Did you honestly think you could get away? Honey, with your height, you couldn't blend in at a Knicks' game, much less out here on the streets."

Holstering her gun, she grabbed his wrists—one at a time—and lowered them behind his back. It was hard to ignore the obvious strength of those wrists and she was at once grateful that he seemed disinclined to put up a struggle. She wrapped the silver cuffs around his thick, masculine wrists and clamped them shut. In the back of her mind she wondered how in the hell she was going to get this nearly seven foot monster into the back of her squad car. She hoped fervently that he didn't suddenly decide to give her any trouble. Her eyes roved over the back of him, from his waist-length auburn hair — shining straight and dark, it was the kind of hair every woman yearned for — to his long legs and large booted feet.

Cautiously, she moved her hand to the stun gun holstered at her leg. She gritted her teeth against a thrill of alarm at his sheer size and obvious strength. If he tried anything she'd be ready to give him a good shock with the TASER in rebuttal. No way was he escaping on her watch — she'd never let one get away yet.

It was why her colleagues revered her so, despite her genteel sex and appearance. She hunted the bad guys down, captured them, and brought them to justice. Every time. Without fail. Once she had the trail of a perp on the run there was no escaping from her. Come hell or high water she was always determined to come out the victor of any battle.

Evidence enough to support her reputation — if anyone ever heard the facts — she'd chased this giant for over two miles before he'd stopped. On foot. She'd have chased him a few more if he hadn't given in to the inevitable and slowed for his arrest. Pride in her work, pride in herself, pride in her position as keeper of the peace would have kept her on his heels, if nothing else, though she was glad he'd surrendered all the same.

But she had to admit to herself — more than pride, it was largely curiosity that drove her now. Curiosity about this mysterious giant in black. Who was he? What was he doing out here on the streets in the middle of the night?

And where in the hell had he learned to throw knives like that?

She'd seen the glint of the streetlights, of the moonlight, reflecting on those blades in his hands as he'd fought his assailants. She'd seen him throw the blades, seen them return to him like razor blade boomerangs. It had been incredible to see. It had also been monumentally dangerous and illegal, which is where she came into the picture.

He'd meant to kill those men. That had been clear enough, and she had to wonder...would he have killed them if she hadn't shown up flashing her badge and her gun? As soon as she'd declared herself and ordered the men to surrender they'd all run from her, keeping to the shadows as if that would keep them safe from her. But this man had followed them, as if he meant to finish what he'd started, no matter that she—a cop—was giving chase.

"Got any needles or weapons in your pockets?" She asked the question out of habit, out of training.

The man didn't respond, merely stood there. Waiting. For what Emily didn't care to know. Let him be stoic while he could...she'd break him down in the interrogation room later.

She patted him down from behind, careful to be wary of any surprises she might find in the folds of his clothing. There were none. All that she found in his pockets were half a dozen tiny glass vials of sludgy black muck—no doubt some new drug she was as yet unfamiliar with.

"Turn around," she ordered.

The man complied and she moved to pat him down from the new angle. Then stopped. The man was practically nude under his coat—covered only in a substance that resembled thick liquid latex. But for his boots, his attire looked painted on over the naked planes of his body. And man oh man, what a body he had under that coat.

Great. Why do I always get the wackos? she thought to herself. It must be because she worked the graveyard shift. They only come out at night.

"Well, we can add public indecency to the list of charges against you," she muttered and proceeded to read him his Miranda Rights.

The man interrupted her, his voice like syrup in her ears. "You might want to get behind me, woman." His words were educated, refined. Oddly cold and warm at the same time, though she couldn't understand or comprehend the combination.

"Are you threatening me, honey?" she asked, raising her eyebrow in a look she knew could bring even the most cold-hearted of men to their knees.

It had taken her nearly thirty-two years to learn how to use her looks and her voice like a weapon. She was a master at it and used it against the black-coated man now, hoping fervently that her backup arrived sooner rather than later.

"No. But they will." He nodded his head in the direction behind her.

She knew better—she was certainly not fool enough to fall for such an old trick—but she looked over her shoulder anyway.

Three hulking men crouched in the shadows there, staring at them.

"Holy shit," she whispered, knowing that something serious was about to happen, whether she wanted it to or not.

One of the men rushed at them, so fast that Emily's heart lurched with instinctive alarm. She wouldn't have time to draw her gun—she knew it with a sick feeling in her stomach. At least her stun gun was already palmed and waiting. Her body went cold and her mind steely as training took over the normal human fear that threatened to spill through her.

But she hadn't counted on the man behind her jumping into the equation. In her preoccupation with the rushing man and his stalking comrades she'd almost forgotten him. Unbelievably foolish and amateurish, she had to admit, though only to herself.

The man moved like lightning to herd her with his body against the wall of the alleyway. Blue-white blades shot out like spiked bracelets around his wrists and his handcuffs fell away in pieces to the ground. Those strange blades of his had cut through the steel like it was butter, though Emily barely had time to gasp over such a wonder. His body pressed back against her violently, penning her in so tightly that she barely had the option of movement, though she struggled like mad to get the stun gun into a position suitable for zapping him without injury to herself.

The man who'd been rushing at them came on, growling and snarling like an animal as he met and clashed with the man in the black coat. Emily leaned around the dark figure to see some of what was going on. A stray sliver of light from a nearby streetlamp illuminated the attacker's face for an instant...but that instant was enough to strike fear and shock into Emily's heart with the force of a hammer's blow.

It was no man after all, but a monster.

A monster!

The form and shape of it was that of a muscular man of above average height, with terrible posture. It was this shape that had fooled her into thinking it was just some rogue criminal or gang member during the chase. But now she saw the slimy, blackened skin. The sharp, dripping fangs. The ten-inch, jagged claws that adorned its overlarge hands.

And the eyes. The glowing orange eyes, bloodshot, bulging and oozing yellow pus… Emily closed her eyes against the horror of it. To see intelligence lurking in the depths of such hellish eyes was to know true terror. If such a thing could exist, could think and possesses self-awareness…then all the gods were surely dead. And the world was truly on its own as so many children of the new millennia had feared.

There was evil in the world of men. And now that Emily knew it she feared she would never feel safe again. All feeling left her, all will to fight or run or do anything. She was, for the first time in her life, stunned beyond belief.

The man ignored her and met the creature head on, but was careful to keep her well protected behind the shield of his back. The bracelet of blue-white spikes disappeared beneath his skin and the creature lunged. The man waved his fingers before the monster's form like a magician and the creature paused, frozen. The man turned to face her and Emily's eyes beheld the sight of the monster falling into slices behind him.

"Stay here, woman. Do not draw their attention further."

"Oh shit," she choked out and gagged, oblivious to the man or his warnings. Her eyes were riveted on the sight of the carnage behind him, by the pile of muck and gore on the ground.

He seemed to sense her momentary lapse of reason and control. While watching the other creatures from the corner of his eye as they now advanced upon them, though much more slowly than the first aggressor, he grabbed her shoulders in his hands, slammed her up against the wall and held her there securely.

He let go of her. A blade, several feet long and winking silver-blue in the dim light, shot out of his wrist. It came free from his flesh, leaving no mark behind to show its passing. Taking the blade between his hands he bent it effortlessly into a U shape, and penned her to the wall with it. He sank the tips of each end deep into the stone on either side of her trembling body.

"Don't move or this will cut you, and it will hurt very badly. Understand?"

His gaze burned into hers, his eyes a clear yellow with flame bursts of orange around the dark pupils. Not entirely dissimilar from those of the monsters' behind him, but where the creatures' eyes were ugly and frightening, his were beautiful and clear and compelling.

He didn't wait for her to respond. With a flap of his black coat he was in the fray. Not one minute had passed since she'd secured the man with her handcuffs, not one minute since she'd been content and comfortable with her view of the world and her place within it. But now everything was changed. Nothing would be the same again.

The man twirled, seeming to glide and fly and dance. Blades projected from his hands and feet like flashes of blue-white light. In and out, in and out, they glinted. He moved so fast the creatures didn't stand a chance against him. Emily's trained eyes couldn't even follow his movements. Within seconds the fight was over and at least four monsters lay dead at his feet—Emily had lost the exact count sometime during the battle.

He came to stand before her, seeming unaffected by the violence he'd just been a part of. "Where did you put my *fl'shan*?"

Fl'shan? What the hell was he talking about? Emily was too confused to reason it out with any success. She, a woman who prided herself on possessing nerves of steel and a stomach for even the worst of crimes, was now a victim of her own fear and doubt.

"You took my *fl'shan* from my pocket. The little vials. Where did you put them?"

"Um…um…in my b-breast pocket," she stuttered.

The man reached out and plunged his long fingers into said pocket. His fingertips brushed over her nipple, which was already hardened due to her freezing fear. The look in his eyes deepened, darkened—an acknowledgement of her femininity—and his fingers lingered perhaps a moment longer than was really necessary.

Her breath hitched and she trembled with fear…and with a desire that was just as terrifying.

"Thank you," he breathed, almost intimately, eyes glowing as he withdrew the vials from her pocket.

He turned and threw the vials onto the street. There was a flash of white flame as they broke. The bodies caught fire quickly, burning hot. White licks of flame rose high and the stench of burning, rotten death assailed her nostrils, making her gag again. She held the contents of her stomach, but only barely, clenching her teeth against the merciless urge to retch.

Turning back, he pulled the blade that imprisoned her out of the wall. He held it aloft in his hand and it straightened as if by magic. It shot back into the flesh at his wrist, sliding out of sight down the length of his arm under his sleeve.

Emily whimpered.

Leaning in close to her, his body almost touching hers, he brought his mouth down until it was a whisper away from hers.

"If you tell anyone what you have seen here tonight, I'll come for you. Do you understand?" His breath was warm against her lips.

She was beyond speech, completely shell-shocked.

"Nod once if you understand."

She nodded, though it took nearly all of her strength to do even so small a thing.

"Good." He reached out and patted her down until he found whatever it was he was searching for. He waved her wallet in front of her face, looked at her I.D., and placed it back into her pocket. "I have your name now. Emily Lansing." He read from her license. "And your address. If you break your faith with me, if you breathe a word of this to anyone—anyone—I will find you. Don't think for a moment that I won't."

And with a flapping of his long, dark coat he was gone.

Emily sank down in the muck of the dark alley, took one look at the ashes of the monsters that scattered the ground before her, and shook like a tree in the cold wind of winter. Her hoarse shout of helpless fear echoed off the brick walls around her. It was a long time before she found the strength to rise. And an even longer time before her shaking eased enough for her to walk away from the battle zone.

When her backup finally arrived, however, there was no way the two male police officers could have guessed that she'd just been given the fright of her life. Calm and collected, professional and knowing, she was the epitome of a jaded cop who'd seen just about everything.

And that was as she preferred.

Chapter One

"What's the matter with you, Emily? You've been really spastic lately…and you look like shit. Not that shit doesn't become you, but it's just weird. You okay?"

"I'm fine, Steve," she said flatly, knowing it was a lie. Steve was right; she did look like shit. And she felt even worse. Seven days without sleep would do that to a person.

"Maybe you need to talk to the counselor? Get some weight off your chest. You've been at this job long enough to be carrying some pretty heavy burdens by now."

"I said I'm fine. I meant it."

Steve smiled. Having worked with her for three years he knew well enough by now to drop the subject. But there was something about her recent behavior that worried him. He wished he knew her better—she was such a guarded, secretive person—so he could get a clearer idea of what was up.

But Emily had always been a loner, standing aloof from those around her. She was a good worker, a great cop with an instinct for danger and nerves of steel…but she was so damned reserved. Steve wondered, not for the first time, if she had any real friends. Any family. He supposed he'd never know.

"Have it your way then. But if you need to talk…"

"Yeah. Thanks," she muttered and went back to her paperwork.

19

Emily waited, holding her breath until Steve left. As a co-worker he wasn't bad. As a friend…well…she'd never needed many of those. It wasn't that she hated people, just that she felt uncomfortable around them most of the time and overall had little use for them. Many were the times she'd been judged harshly because of her innocent looks yet not so innocent mind. As a whole, or so she'd come to believe, people were often frightened of what they couldn't understand.

Most people didn't understand her at all.

When she was silent or shy she was judged as cold or stuck-up. When she was vocal she was found to be rude or aggressive for her tendency to be overly blunt. At work, she was as serious as they came. Her work was her life and she firmly believed in the system. But not everyone was as dedicated as she, and many saw her as a threat to their position in the force. She was shunned. And she did her own fair share of shunning—if only to avoid further conflicts. It was just how she dealt with things.

She was, at best, a loner. Only a rare few had looked beyond her exterior to the woman that lay beneath the surface. Only a rare few could she really call friend. And that was fine enough with her.

Her head swam with weariness. Her stomach lurched from lack of food. But she'd been too edgy to sleep this past week. Too preoccupied with dark thoughts to do more than eat whatever small fare was at hand.

The memory of wicked fangs and claws and monstrous growls consumed her mind now. Visions of a tall man in a dark trench coat with long, shining hair swam in her tired eyes. It had been a week since that night in the alley—a week since her world had been turned on its axis. And still she felt the fear.

The shame.

Shame because she'd succumbed to her weaker impulses. Given in to her fear, her terror. It had never happened to her before; she'd never allowed it. But in the face of such alien evil she'd lost her wits, gagged, trembled and weakened. It was not to be borne. Emily vowed it would never happen again, even under pain or fear of death.

She looked out the window on the far side of her station, situated as it was in the middle of the receiving lobby. The dawn was streaking its warm, strawberry rays over the sky beyond the glass, the edges of the night fleeing in a stain of pink and gold and blue. It was summertime. The dawn came to the world early now, and she would leave work with its cheerful shine this morning.

Hopefully she'd be able to sleep today. Insomnia could only last so long, after all. And she should know, being a poster child for the sleepless community. Her entire life had been peppered with bouts of insomnia. It was just one of her many quirks, though it had never plagued her for so long a stretch without even a light doze.

The world around her was lost in a marshmallow haze during times like this. Like a canvas of wet oils that had slid off its easel to splash its ocean of color onto the floor, her tired eyes saw only the vague outline of reality's normally crisp picture. Everything was surreal. Nothing was as it should be. Colors, textures, scents, tastes and even emotions...all held but an echo of their usual brilliance when she went too long without sleep.

At times she wondered if the monsters and the man in the black coat had been hallucinations after all. Horrific visions dredged from the depths of a sleep-deprived brain. Wouldn't that be wonderful? But unfortunately she knew better. Her insomnia had set in after the attack. Had been brought on because of it. But it was fun to pretend—to wish—in her weaker moments, that it had all been a waking dream.

She hadn't told anyone, of course. Not really because of the man's threat to come after her if she did, but because she knew no one would believe her. Knew it would, in fact, put her job and her reputation on the line if she spoke of the monsters without proof of their existence. And that she could not bear, even to tell the truth. She'd worked too hard for too long to lose it all simply because her tale would be too fantastical to believe.

So what was left to her?

Not much. Her life was forever altered after that experience in the alley. Her drive to be a peacekeeper, a protector of the people, had been redirected along a new path without her even wanting it to be. Common thugs no longer concerned her full time as they had but a week before. Now she knew there were far more dangerous threats stalking the dark streets of the night. And she couldn't let that go as if it had never happened. She had to do something about it.

Instinctively she knew there were more of those evil creatures out there. Knew that, despite his threatening words to the contrary, the man in the black coat had been on her side. If indeed he was a man. He'd been so strange, with his blades shooting out from his very flesh, and his dangerous fiery eyes. She wouldn't be surprised at this juncture to learn that he'd been something other than a man. An alien perhaps?

God, had she really lost it? Had she snapped? She needed to get away, to think for a while of a way to best meet this new threat. There would be no real rest for her until she solved this puzzle or was driven mad by it.

Which was why she'd asked for a two-week leave. Since she'd never in her five years on the force taken a sick day, or even a vacation day, her boss had given her the time with no questions asked. Hopefully that time would be enough for her to come to grips with the harsh new reality that threatened to push her into madness. Perhaps she'd find a way to redeem her cowardice in the alley…if only for her own ego's sake.

And maybe she'd finally get some sleep.

Grabbing her things she rose from her desk and bid farewell to the necessary people. The warm welcome of the summer morning greeted her with a perfumed heat— the scent of blooming morning flowers light in the air. Crawling into her car with a weary weight in her bones, she headed for her home, and the adventure she knew would either spell her doom or salvation.

* * * * *

Even the warmth of her bath couldn't lull her to sleep, though her body so desperately craved its sweet oblivion. But it did, nevertheless, feel good to her screaming muscles. It seemed that the longer she stayed awake, the more her muscles strained against themselves. She ached from head to toe. Even pulling her hairbrush through her hair was a painful chore.

Clothing hurt her skin—ravaged it. Her nerves were sensitive, aching and screaming from sleep deprivation. She opted to crawl into her bed nude, leaving her bathwater to dry negligently on her skin. She kicked the bed covers onto the floor and tossed and turned, looking for the perfect position in which to seek her rest. Nothing seemed comfortable. No position had a natural feel, so she finally flopped onto her back, huffing in grumpy agitation.

Emily ran her hands over the damp curves of her body, trying to soothe away the tension. A flash of memory, of the sight of the tall man's body covered in ebony liquid latex under his coat, assailed her mind. Her breathing hitched. It was as good a fantasy as any, she supposed, and ran her hands over the peaking tips of her breasts.

She hadn't been afforded much of a look at him, had only seen the muscled line of his chest and stomach and thigh, barely covered in the latex. But she had a good imagination and filled in the blanks where she wished. His skin would be gold where hers was alabaster. His body would be strong and tall and heavy against her much smaller, delicate frame.

The pain in her muscles ebbed and dulled, replaced by the tingling warmth of desire.

His mouth would taste of heaven. His eyes...she turned away from the memory of them. She wanted no closer knowledge of the man in the black coat, even in fantasy. He oozed danger...and where he dwelled in her mind, so too did the monsters. Better he be a faceless phantom lover with the body of a god than the dark angel, the warrior, she knew him to be.

The long silk of his rich auburn hair would fall across her body, caressing her like thousands of tiny kisses. It would tangle in the blue-black curls that fell about her own shoulders as they moved together. His muscles would be smooth, hairless and glistening. His cock would be thick and long and demanding.

Her hands moved over the smooth plane of her stomach, down to the mound of wet flesh between her legs. The image of his hand replacing hers made her gasp with longing. It was easy for her to imagine him parting her folds, seeking out the swell of her clit and rubbing it expertly, as she was doing.

Spreading her legs wide so that her dream lover would have the room to settle his bulk between them, she bucked her hips against the burn of his cock and fingers. She sighed. Her pussy was so wet, so swollen and tender that she cried out with each press of her dream lover's body against her. His finger filled her, fucked her roughly, mercilessly, until she was panting and rocking against him.

The fingers on her clit rubbed in a circular pattern and she grew impossibly wetter. Creamier. But it wasn't enough. The fantasy faded. She growled and thrashed her head on her pillow. She needed to be filled. Stretched. Impaled.

Emily reached into the drawer of her nightstand and retrieved her dual action vibrator. Without preamble she thrust it deep into her pussy and turned it on. She wanted it hard. Needed it hard and fast and frenzied. Merciless vibrations beat at her clit and she sighed. The thick length of the soft latex shaft filled her, moving in small circles deep within her, rubbing against her G-spot with each rotation it made. She smiled and fell back, thrusting the vibrator in and out of her wetness with a dreamy moan, letting the magic of it sweep over her.

It was easy to fall back into fantasy. To imagine it was he filling her, fucking her with his long, thick cock. That it was he who rubbed her clit until it throbbed and swelled, not the vibrator. She heard the sucking sounds her pussy made as he thrust in and out of her, felt the hard slap of him against her as he moved.

It was his voice that brought her over the edge. The memory of that dark, smooth voice—fire and ice combined—that made her lose control at last. She imagined him whispering dirty, risqué promises in her ear. Imagined him telling her how luscious her cunt was, how hot and wet it felt while wrapped around him. Imagined him growling out how tasty her nipples were, how much he wanted—needed—to fuck her.

She cried out, trembling and bucking on the bed. The force of her climax swept through her like a tidal wave. She tingled from head to toe. Her nipples and clit were like throbbing stars in a heaven of pleasure. It was all consuming. It lasted for long, endless moments. And when she came back down she had a small, satisfied smile playing about her lips. She could feel it there and almost laughed at herself.

For hours she lay there, spent and languorous in her bed. The day came and went and then nightfall was again sweeping across the world.

But still she couldn't sleep.

Chapter Two

"After months of quiet the Horde is now making a move into New York City. Why? There must be some reason."

"I don't know, Elder, but I've met them twice in the past week. And each time there are more."

"Have you heard from Obsidian yet, Traveler? Have they found any activity on their patrols?"

"Not that I know of. Shall I call the team to us?"

"Do you need their aid?" Tryton asked.

The Traveler and Edge exchanged glances—though Edge couldn't really see The Traveler's eyes beyond the shadow of his cowl. It didn't matter. He understood the sentiment behind their silent communication.

"Not yet," Edge answered, turning back to The Elder. "Thus far they have been relatively easy to defeat. I will wait until I know more about this threat before seeking my teammates' assistance."

"You are, as always, a formidable warrior, Edge. But if you encounter too dire a threat I want you to return here immediately. I will not have your life placed in too much danger unnecessarily. Though your team is spread thin to cover more ground in the Territories, you are still dependent on each other for full strength. Your team will be summoned to help you if the Horde makes a strong move. Is that clear?"

"Of course, Elder." Edge bowed to his leader respectfully.

"Traveler, you will remain by his side as much as possible. I do not want Edge to find himself without hope of escape should the situation grow too desperate."

The Traveler nodded his acceptance of Tryton's direction.

"Now if you'll both excuse me. The Council awaits."

Tryton exited the room, leaving the two men alone.

"The woman. Have you seen her again?" The Traveler asked, breaking the silence.

"No. She was just a lone law enforcement official, no threat to us. Give her no more thought." He'd do well to follow his own advice, he thought, with no small amount of chagrin. Truth was, he'd thought of little else since running into the woman.

"I find I cannot help thinking on her. And on the Daemons' untimely arrival in her city."

"What are you getting at?"

But The Traveler didn't answer. Instead, he retreated from the room in silence, following Tryton's footsteps.

Travelers and their secretive ways had always gotten on Edge's nerves. But now…he wondered what occupied The Traveler's thoughts. Wondered where the woman with the gorgeous crimson baby's mouth and glossy curls fit in with the man's ponderings concerning the Horde. He didn't like knowing that she was the object of The Traveler's attention. Didn't like knowing that the man dwelled on her, even for a second's passing.

Didn't like it at all.

* * * * *

Armed to the teeth and sporting her bulletproof vest as a precaution in addition to the weight of her weapons, Emily prowled around the streets of the city's underbelly in search of her nightmare. But the creatures, thus far, were nowhere to be found.

Drugs, prostitution, and thievery abounded here. While not being as dangerous as many other cities, this one had its fair share of darkness and secrets. If one knew where to look. And she did.

But the monsters were elusive. Or else they didn't really exist.

God, she was tired. But on she walked, trudging through the dank and dirty streets in search of redemption. Redemption for the moment of weakness she'd shown in the face of the threat of evil. A threat she should have faced head on, instead of cowering before it in a stupor of fear.

After hours of research, in the library and on the Internet, Emily still had no solid information about her prey. What were they? Why were they here? And how long had they hidden in the shadows, undetected by virtually anyone who would be willing—or able—to catalogue what they saw, leaving clues for others to find? In fact no book or website had given her any leads...save one.

TheVoyeurs.net

An odd link she'd found buried in FTP sites and encrypted file searches, Emily had first thought it to be one of the endless porn sites dotted about the Net because of its name. But the page was so well hidden that she'd wondered about it and finally typed in the address to see what info it might divulge, if any.

It was a surprise to find exactly what she had been looking for, if a little too vague to be entirely useful. The website was run by college students — all female — with an interest in the paranormal. They asked for photos and sighting reports of the beasts they'd nicknamed Daemons — from the Latin Daemonio for 'evil demon' — and promised in-depth study of the phenomena. Though there were photos and a few forum posts on the subject there hadn't been much to go on besides the expected ufology-styled speculation of the site itself.

Finally obtaining some proof — however small — that she wasn't the only witness to these monsters, these Daemons, she felt a lot less ridiculous about searching for them. Also, she now had some ideas of how to kill the beasts. 'Take their heart and burn their hide' had been the only real instruction on the website. Though fighting the Daemons was strongly cautioned against all throughout the domain. Study and report, but do not engage had been the motto and the rule.

It would seem, however, that sometimes skirmishes were unavoidable for the web mistresses to offer such dangerous instructions in addition to their warnings.

Now Emily could either take the website at face value and follow their advice, or find out for herself just what these so called Daemons were made of. If they existed to be found, she would find them. And she would do what she must to protect the citizens of her city from their threat. It was a driving force within her, this need to serve and protect. It always had been. And, despite all the endless stringent rules involved in police work, she'd taken up the badge with that very purpose in mind. To keep the streets safe from danger and crime.

Many times over she could have taken a desk job. Many times over she'd turned down promotion after promotion, instead wanting—needing—to patrol the streets. She liked knowing that she made a difference, liked to see the results of her own handiwork. Duty and honor, these were the most important things in her life and had been for longer than she could remember.

Sitting on the steps of a rickety old fire escape, she released a heavy expulsion of breath. Her muscles trembled with fatigue. Her bones felt rubbery beneath her skin and her head felt swollen atop her sagging shoulders. The sound of a lone wolf howling came from a distance. But there were no wolves in New York. Lone or otherwise.

"I've totally lost it," she whispered to herself. "Totally."

There was another noise in the darkness. Close this time. It was brief and almost inaudible, but she heard it nonetheless. A sift of dust fell down over her head, light and weightless. She would have missed it if she hadn't been so edgy. Her hand crept towards the handgun holstered at her waist, slowly, cautiously so as to be undetectable to anyone who might be watching from overhead.

It was probably just some poor, homeless soul perched above her on the fire escape. She just hadn't seen their shadowy form when she'd taken her seat. Holding on to that thought, she palmed her Glock 23—a sturdy, dependable weapon—and instinctively steadied her nerves.

The smell of refuse, rotten and ripe, was thick in the air. Had she noticed it before? Or had it only just crept into her sensory field? The scent thickened, turned to one of death — a sickly sweet perfume — of fleshly decay.

She daren't look above her. To do so would give away her only advantage of surprise. The person — or thing — above her must not know she was aware of its presence. As an added precaution, her free hand inched towards another pistol, fastened to the outside of her thigh. She shifted just so, to hide her movements. To mask her intent.

Another shift of mass above her sent a shower of dirt down onto her head. She flew into motion, her training taking over the command of her muscles as if her higher brain were on autopilot. Raising her weapons high she jerked out from under the fire escape, turned as swift as a thought, and faced the threat that waited above her.

A large, scruffy cat meowed plaintively at her from the level above where she'd been sitting. Emily laughed at herself, exhaled her pent up breath, and lowered her weapons. "I'm way too paranoid tonight," she said with another shaky chuckle.

Two massive, clawed hands clamped down like iron vises on her shoulders.

Emily jumped, fear taking hold of her completely, utterly. But luck was with her, as well as her training. She ducked, bringing her pistols up above her head with incredible speed. She fired point blank into the chin of the hulking monster behind her. The creature's head exploded as the bullet exited the back of its skull, and it wobbled on its feet like a drunkard.

But it did not fall.

Before she even knew what she intended, she emptied both pistols into the creature. The chest and belly of the headless monstrosity was ravaged by the force of the bombardment and at last the creature faltered, lost its footing, and fell back onto the ground.

It was pure instinct that had her immediately reloading her weapons.

"I should have brought a damned shotgun," she muttered. "Or two." The mundane words calmed her a bit, helped her to find her scattered wits.

The body on the ground twitched, as if it were still animated by the unnamed hellish force that drove it. But how could it still be alive, after all the damage it had taken? It was impossible. Wasn't it?

There came the sound of a low-pitched and vicious growl behind her. She whirled, raising her weapon, and fired immediately upon the new threat. Two of the creatures came for her, slow and clumsy when she knew firsthand that they could move swiftly and dangerously. Mere seconds ticked by and her guns were once more emptied of ammunition.

Would knives destroy them more quickly, more completely than guns? The man in the black coat had used those strange blades to destroy the creatures...perhaps steel was the answer. She pulled two wicked hunting knives out of her boots—one for each hand. No way did she want to get close enough to the things to use them...but she had to find out how best to defeat them.

At least she had the advantage now, as these brutal things were riddled with ragged holes from her hail of bullets.

Bracing her hands tightly around the hilt of the blades, she advanced upon the creatures. The smell of carrion grew thicker as she drew closer. It took all of her courage, her strength, to meet them. But she did. She had to. Or else she could never face herself in the mirror again.

Using every ounce of strength she possessed, she brought one of the knives up and buried into the belly of the closest monster. Ripping it from belly to neck, she laid it open with a brutality she had no inkling she'd possessed. The creature screamed, a hellish cry, and fell back.

The remaining monster seemed to rally its wits in an effort to face her with more success. Its eyes, so horrible to behold, held a glimmer of human intelligence that sent a shaft of icy dread and fear into Emily's heart. It backed away from Emily with much caution. Slowly, it began to circle her, and she was careful to keep her eyes locked to it while it moved.

Fighting a monster was not the same as fighting a human foe, though the creature did possess humanoid qualities. While in combat with a human, Emily could judge through body language and involuntary muscle contraction, just how or when a person may attack. But with this creature it was nearly impossible to judge, beneath all the muck and slime of its flesh, just how its muscles reacted during motion. And its body language was so alien, so freakishly monstrous, that she had no idea what it intended beyond the moment at hand.

It seemed cautious, crouching as it moved as if it might pounce...or flee. It was impossible to tell. Emily felt its evil, its rotten core. And yet it seemed to possess nothing but the most basic of intents and purposes. Like an infant trapped in the body of a murdering adult. It was unsettling. Disturbing. And Emily couldn't fathom it.

Where in many instances she could understand, perhaps pity, human criminals, she couldn't connect at all with this hellish being. It had no business in her world — this much she knew for certain. And so she would dispatch it to whatever pit of hell it had crawled out of. But she would feel no remorse in doing so.

There was no way she was going to let it escape, to bedevil or endanger someone else in her fair city.

"Emily," the monster gurgled.

She started and almost vomited on herself, so great was her fear and revulsion of that vile voice speaking her name. How could it possibly know her name? Oh God.

"What the fuck are you?" She spoke first in a whisper, then repeated her words in a shout full of rage and fear, shaking uncontrollably with the force of her emotions. "What the fuck are you?"

"Emily," it spoke again. "Come."

"No way, you sick shit, no way." Out of fear — fear for herself and for the faceless people of her city — she darted towards it, knife at the ready to mete out death.

The creature's arms came around her, tried to hold her. But she took it to the ground, plunging the blade deep into its chest. At the same moment, the monster whose intestines she'd ripped asunder, came and joined the fray. Emily shrieked in disbelief. "Why won't you die?" She yelled as the second monster came and grabbed her arm in a brutal grip, trying no doubt to drag her off its comrade.

She struck out wildly with her blades, slicing flesh to ribbons until she and her foes were covered in the thick wet heat of their black blood. It took much wrestling but she broke free of their cloying embrace as they sought to hold her to them…for what purpose she couldn't say.

But she knew that they were holding back from injuring her. Many times over they could have sank their claws deep into her, ending the fight. But they didn't. For some reason—no doubt nefarious—they held back, even under pain and threat of their own demise. Emily knew it—could sense their refusal to fully meet her blow for blow. This knowledge struck an endless terror into her heart.

What did they want with her?

Emily retreated, adrenaline flooding her body. The monsters were clumsier now, proving that they were weakened by their wounds, if only a little. It proved they weren't impervious to her weapons…only very resistant. She knew they could die, she'd seen the man kill them with effortless ease.

What had she missed? What had he done that she had failed to do?

Fire. She needed fire with which to burn them. Only in the heat of the flames had they failed to rise again. And the website—which she hadn't taken seriously enough by half it now seemed—had also said to kill them with fire.

With a clumsy hand she dropped one of her knives and searched her pockets for a lighter. She was no smoker, but a good officer never entered the field unprepared for everything that might occur. Or, at least, she didn't. An old, silver lighter rested in her back pocket, coming into her hands when she reached for it, as if it had been waiting for her the whole time.

A knife clutched in one hand, the lighter in the other, she advanced upon the creatures once more. The flame of her lighter, however small, flickered and reflected off the yellow of their eyes. They cried out and retreated, at last giving her the advantage.

"You're scared of the fire, aren't you?" she murmured, gathering her courage as she realized the truth of her own words. "You know what it will do to you."

The monsters almost tripped over themselves in an effort to get away. Even the headless one on the ground twitched, though it was too brutally injured to get up and flee with the others. As Emily stepped over it, she bent down and set the small lick of flame to the creature's flesh.

And almost singed her eyebrows off in the doing. The thing caught fire so fast! Seconds only—that's all it took before the body was completely engulfed in flame.

"Burn, baby, burn," she whispered, stepping past it in pursuit of the still slowly retreating monsters.

"What are you? Where have you come from?" she asked them as she backed them into a corner. "I know you can speak. You spoke my name. How did you know my name? Tell me, damn it, or you'll burn like your friend." Her words were a torrent, fast and breathless, from both fear and the adrenaline rushing unchecked through her veins.

But the creatures only growled their response, the sound inching its way into her soul like the stain of blackest hate.

"Fine. Go back to the hell you came from, then." Keeping her eyes on them, she reached down to retrieve a piece of trash that littered the ground at their feet. Setting fire to the torn piece of newspaper, she advanced, brandishing the makeshift torch at them...

And gasped to see them disappear completely before the fire could even touch them.

"What the...?" She looked about her frantically, fearing a sudden reappearance and attack at her back. But the alley was empty. Empty but for the smoldering corpse of the first monster as it burned to ash.

What had happened? How had they disappeared like that?

Whatever the answers to her endless — and growing — list of questions, Emily vowed to find them out. Even if it killed her.

Chapter Three
Five nights later

Emily grunted as she dragged the last corpse onto the pyre. Her muscles were beyond weary. Beyond fatigued. With a grimy hand, she wiped away the sweat that poured from her brow. Her gaze swept the carnage that surrounded her. A pile of the monsters' hearts burned almost cheerily in a corner of the abandoned building — a decrepit factory that had been old long before she was born.

It had been on the third night that she'd discovered for herself that what the voyeurs website claimed had been truth. The monsters' true weakness lay in their hearts. It was their beating heart that kept their bodies animated. So long as the heart survived, the body would go on fighting — no matter how many pieces it may be in at the time. In every fight before then, when she was fast enough to incapacitate them before they disappeared, she'd just burned them as she could. Whether they stood or crawled or still fought, she torched them as quickly as possible.

But on that third night she'd ravaged a monster, practically pulverized its body into a pile of goo with blasts from her shotgun. But its heart had somehow survived, and it had beat a terrible tattoo in the cage of crushed ribs that uselessly strove to protect it. Emily had studied it, watching its terrible rhythm with horror and curiosity...and the wreck that was the body had moved! It was then that she remembered the website's instruction; it was then that she had known.

To kill the beast one must take its heart.

So now, instead of pummeling the creatures with an endless arsenal of ammunition, she took their hearts as quickly as she could. Their chests were soft, spongy and weak. It was almost too easy to take their hearts from them, now that she knew to strike there first.

It also helped that they still refused to actually hurt her.

Emily used this against them every chance she got. She still had no idea why they refrained from causing her a debilitating injury. It certainly wasn't out of any goodness or charity on their parts. They were evil beasts, of that there could be no doubt.

She'd seen them feed.

Seen them eating a body. Seen and heard them as they'd crunched down to the last bone of their hellish meal. Emily had been far too late to save the victim, but she'd vowed to never allow such an atrocity to happen on her watch again. Those monsters had died most horribly and she'd reveled in the torture she'd inflicted on them, taking them apart one piece at a time. But their black deed had proven one thing, at least. That she was on the side of right. Of good.

The world was in danger. And she was more than ready to help fight against that danger, to help keep people safe.

Taking a deep breath, knowing that the air around her was about to be poisoned with the pungent scent of the monsters' burning flesh, she threw a match onto the pile of bodies and watched as it burned. Several minutes later, after the evidence of her fight had been reduced to harmless ash, she gathered her weapons to her and went in search of yet another battle.

Thunder rolled in the heavens as a storm approached, but Emily was too tired to notice or care.

* * * * *

It was raining so heavily that his coat dragged about him like a dead weight. Thankfully the liquid polymer paint Steffy and Agate had designed for his battles was completely waterproof, serving as a rain slicker as well as armor. With his speed and precision he could walk between the raindrops, but that would have taken more concentration than he had to spare at the moment. For at this moment he was hunting Daemons.

He was no member of the Hunter Caste—Shikars gifted with the uncanny ability to sense and track Daemons over great distances—but he was close enough to his quarry now to sense their location. He felt the dread that seemed to permeate the air whenever they were close by. Felt the stain they left behind when they Traveled from their world to this. And these feelings, these Shikar perceptions, drove him to increase his pace down the seemingly endless secret back streets of the city.

They were uncomfortably close. What could they want so desperately here, to keep coming back for it in such a hostile land as this? Did the monsters no longer fear discovery and human mob panic? Were there so many psychics to be found in this great human city? It must be so, to lure them back night after night, when they could have hunted less developed, less populated lands as this with much greater ease.

Edge turned one last corner and it was then that he came upon them. But it was the other — the woman — whose presence surprised him most. And he was a man intolerant of surprises.

It was the policewoman, though now she did not wear the uniform of her station. Emily Lansing, of the glorious shiny curls, and rose red child's mouth. Emily of the cobalt blue eyes, eyes so deep and so purely blue as to shine like precious jewels in her peaches-and-cream face. And though Edge's libido immediately awoke in response to her presence, his cock growing heavy and thick and hard just at the sight of her, he was not in the least otherwise happy to see her.

The human had no business being here. And what was she doing, anyway?

She was fighting the Daemons.

Emily brought up a large black handgun and blew a hole into the chest of the nearest Daemon and Edge watched, amazed, as she immediately reached in with a gloved hand and ripped out the heart of the beast. Her movements were like those of the most seasoned warrior, striking out in the deadliest and most dangerous of ways as each of the four monsters moved to advance upon her.

She was hopelessly outnumbered. Any moment now a Daemon would surely reach out and tear her life from her.

The thought pushed Edge to immediate and swift action. Releasing a row of seven deadly, poison-tipped Foils down his forearm — ripping wide holes in his painted-on sleeves as he did so — he leapt into the fray. Swinging wide, he tore into the torso of one of his foes with his bladed arm, leaving a gory maw behind. Reaching out he grabbed the creature's heart in his fist, before kicking the monster back with the flat of one boot. The force of his blow sent the Daemon flying and Edge moved on to the next enemy, crushing the heart in his fist as he did so.

The rain was a torrent, flooding the ground around them. The storm's violence matched theirs, but was no help because of it. The rain made a dense curtain, difficult to see through. There were now two Daemons left standing and as they turned to run from the warriors, the rain served as a shield to hide them while they fled. Edge pursued, his Shikar eyes able to see through the rain far better than Emily could have hoped to.

But the Daemons were strong in their fear, and they managed to Travel their way out of Edge's path, disappearing into thin air so that Edge had no hope of following.

"Damn it." He growled the words impotently, looking about him in what he knew was a vain hope of spotting them. They were gone. And no doubt they wouldn't be back until they had some reinforcements.

When Edge retraced his steps it was to find Emily crouched over a pile of Daemon bodies, trying with unsteady fingers to light a soaking wet match. She'd removed her gloves so that the smallness of her fingers looked like those of a child, and certainly no stronger. She looked up at him, and until that moment he'd been unsure if she'd even noticed him during the battle.

"I can't set a blaze in all this rain." She said it flatly, as if it were perfectly natural for her to be crouched over the corpses of her Daemon kills, attempting to set fire to their remains.

Edge's temper got the better of him, he who had never been one to fall victim to emotion—be they his or someone else's. He reached into the folds of his coat, grabbed some vials of *fl'shan* and then threw them on the corpses. Flames engulfed the pyre and the woman scrambled backwards on all fours, eyes wide.

"Just what in the name of the Horde are you doing, human?" he roared down into her face.

Emily's eyes narrowed to dangerous blue slits and she rose slowly to face him. She was small, perhaps no bigger than five-two, and slender besides. The rain made thick locks of her blue-black hair, streaming it down into her face, lending her a truly vulnerable look despite her proud stance. Her size, her coloring—everything about her pleased the eye. But she seemed too angry to realize how appealing a picture she presented to him now.

"I could ask you the same thing. But I know for a fact you're not human. Which leaves the question—whose side are you on? Mine? Theirs? Yours?"

"What about you? Are you on the side of good or evil?" he countered.

Emily raised the barrel of a shotgun. "Good. Bad. I'm the one with the gun. I'll be asking the questions, if you don't mind."

Edge reached out with a hand that suddenly sported wicked razor Foils at the fingertips. Moving far faster than she could see, he sliced through the barrel of the gun, sending it falling to pieces on the wet ground at their feet. Emily rolled her eyes, her exasperated response surprising him, and twisted her small tender mouth into a sneer.

"You gonna pay for that?"

"Humans," he muttered before moving against her. One moment he was staring down into the beautiful face that had haunted his dreams since their first meeting, the next he was hauling her up with rough hands against a brick wall. "Why are you here? You could have easily been killed."

"Not so easily as you might think," she countered, spraying droplet of rain into his face as her lips moved around the words.

"I should lay you over my knee and tan your hide for being so foolish. Don't you know the danger you're in? Don't you have a care for your own life?"

"My life wouldn't matter much if I just stood back and let these things run around killing people. I have to do something. I have to help."

He shook her there against the wall. "If you died your life wouldn't be worth much anyway."

Her sapphire eyes bored into his, seeming to steal past every shield he possessed, to see into the depths of his very soul. "What about you? You could die just as easily as I could...or can't you die?"

"I'm not immortal. But it is my duty to fight these things. You have no business here. I do."

"I have more business than you. I'm a human and I am protecting my fellow humans. It's my duty too, now." Her eyes were as stubbornly hard as the jewels they resembled.

The rain beat down on their heads. Edge bowed his head, knowing he would never be able to gather his thoughts if he kept looking into her eyes and was surprised to note that he held Emily completely off the ground. Her feet dangled. Neither of them had noticed, it seemed.

Her hands caught in his wet, tangled hair and pulled his face back up to hers. Heaven didn't possess the blue color of her eyes as her gaze roved over his face. He felt the firm press of her bulletproof vest as she drew him slowly closer. Her intent was clear. That childlike mouth pressed against his, feeling softer than down, smooth as silk. Lush and full, its weight was exquisite against his.

He gave in to her allure.

Emily wasn't thinking; she was only feeling. The need to kiss him was so great that she had no hope of fighting against it. Heart pounding, knees weak, she kissed him with all the passion that was in her. He tasted like danger. Like sex, pure and wet and hot. And he tasted like man. So much man that her senses swam. She was drunk on lust. On desire. On him.

Slanting his lips down upon hers, he ravaged them. He sucked their fullness into his mouth. He licked and bit and nuzzled against them. His hands almost shook as he drew one of his long, razor-sharp foils down the front of his suit. He wanted to be nude against her, wanted his skin against hers the soonest. It was easy work to peel the remnants of his covering away.

Drawing her to him in a crushing embrace, he deepened the kiss. Pressing his body against hers made them both gasp in pleasure. Emily wrapped her legs around his waist, and he cupped the fullness of her buttocks in his large hands. His tongue touched hers, slid deep within her mouth to get a better taste, and feasted.

As aggressive as he, Emily put her hands beneath his coat, to stroke and test his bare muscled chest. She undulated—hard—against his cock as it strained against her heat. Moans escaped her mouth only to be swallowed by his. She used her teeth to nibble and to bite, against his lips and tongue. Emily wanted to eat him in her passion.

At last she broke away from him and pressed desperate kisses to the strong line of his jaw and neck. His skin was so smooth, so firm as if he'd only just shaved. The rain slicked them both, but it did nothing to dampen his scent. She breathed it deep and moaned. He smelled so glorious, so delicious. Spicy and woodsy and clean and sweet—all separate and together at the same time. It was an orgasmic experience just to breathe him in.

Her fingers clutched him to her. His hands kneaded and separated her buttocks, bringing her against him in thrusting motions that mimicked coitus perfectly. Emily wanted him inside of her and she wanted him there now.

Pulling back, she went to work on her clothing as best she could while still in his arms. He followed her, reclaiming her mouth with his, blanking her mind. He hitched her more securely against him and held her with one hand. The other moved around to her front. His mouth released hers and they looked down.

He moved the tip of one long finger down the middle of her chest. There was the flash of a blade. Her nipples hardened as they were exposed to the air. He had cut through her shirt, through her vest, through her bra. Her skin was unharmed as her clothing fell away in tatters and she arched her breasts up against him shamelessly.

The blade that protruded from his finger stroked erotically against her, though how he kept from cutting her she couldn't have guessed. The thrill of that danger was there, between them, heightening her desire. He traced the pout of her breast and nipple until it swelled and trembled. Emily moaned and ground her hips against the heavy heat of his erection, hopelessly caught up in the most basic of her sleep-deprived instincts. The need to mate.

Her hands shook, with both desire and excitement, upon the fastenings of her jeans. But again his hand was there to help. A few swift motions and she was naked against him, her jeans in tatters around her ankles. The rain soaked her flesh but she was too full of hot desire to feel its chill. Emily reached down between their bodies and grasped his thick sex in her hand. He was large, heavy, and long.

And she wanted every last, thick inch of him.

"Fuck me. Please fuck me," she moaned against his mouth.

He needed no more urging. His long fingers came between them, testing her readiness, finding her nearly dripping with her own need. The broad head of his cock slipped into position between the swollen lips of her cunt.

Their eyes met and burned.

He thrust home in one long, smooth move.

Emily screamed her pleasure-pain aloud in the rain. But she did not pull away. With desperate hands she clutched him more tightly to her, clawing him until not even the rainwater came between their skin. He was still within her, stretching her, penetrating her to her very heart. And he waited patiently, seeming to be waiting for her to adjust to his strength, to the wicked depth of his penetration.

Emily was far too impatient to wait. Tightening her legs around his waist, she began to ride him. It was rough and awkward at first—she'd never been with so large a man—but it was exquisite all the same. And when his hands came around to help guide her movements it seemed she would die from the pleasure, it was so great. But it still wasn't enough.

"Harder. Harder. Bruise me. Make me feel…" she wailed brokenly, in between the small screams that escaped her lips each time he thrust home.

His body slammed into hers. Her teeth jarred from the force of his deep thrusts. Her nails dug into his broad shoulders and she kissed him with deep, licking strokes of her tongue into his mouth. She wanted to swallow him, with her mouth and with her body, until they were truly one being. Never in her life had she felt like this, in thrall to her most basic emotions and needs. The unrelenting force of them should have frightened her. But she felt only the rage of her desire as it burned through her veins like the headiest of drugs.

She let it take them both in a rush that could have drowned them.

The wall at her back scraped with delicious pain against her flesh. The deep wet well of her body trembled around his length and he must have felt it because his movements grew fiercer, faster. With his thumb he found her clit and rubbed it with expert caresses. She pressed herself more tightly against him and she felt the strong pounding rhythm of his heart like some primitive drum in his chest.

When she came, the pulses of her orgasm matched that rhythm perfectly.

"Ohgodohgodohgod." She cried unintelligible words into his mouth as he brought her.

It was so powerful, her release. Her orgasm was so strong that her teeth would have clenched against it if his tongue hadn't been filling her mouth. The whole length of her body shuddered and bucked and undulated against his in wild abandon. An entire army of monsters could have attacked them in that moment and she wouldn't have cared, for she had found heaven.

And heaven would not be denied.

When at last she came down from her dance with the angels, she again felt the aches and discomforts of her weary body. Her eyes grew heavy, so heavy that she couldn't keep them open. Her head was a dead weight that she had to rest against his strong shoulder.

Sleep came at last, stealing over her like a thief in the night. There in the arms of a man whose name she did not know, but whose body had given her such a sweet oblivion, she at last found her rest.

And it was the sweetest she'd ever known.

* * * * *

Emily's eyes felt gluey when she finally managed to open them. The sun was setting beyond her bedroom windows. The man in the black coat must have taken her home after she'd fallen asleep in his arms—she certainly didn't remember making her own way back. Amazingly, she'd slept the whole day through—the first decent sleep she'd had in more days than she cared to number.

As groggy as she was it took her several long moments to remember all of the events of the previous evening. When she did, she groaned with embarrassment. Had she really been that aggressive? Had she really begged the man—a stranger whose name she still did not know — to fuck her? She had. And though the interlude had been glorious, the most amazing sex she'd ever had, she couldn't help feeling chagrined by her own uninhibited behavior.

What must he think of her? Would he, like any other man might in his position, feel she'd given free access to her body indefinitely? Would he expect more of the same from her when next they met? Would he be angry when she told him, in plain terms, that she hadn't been herself last night? That their coupling had been a mistake on her part, never to be repeated again? Her mind was a storm of such questions.

Emily fully intended to meet with him again. She wanted to learn more about him, about who and what he was. Not for personal reasons, she reassured herself — deliberately ignoring the excitement she felt at the mere thought of meeting him again — but for professional ones.

It was obvious to her now that wherever the monsters were he would no doubt be nearby. So her nightly hunt would now have two purposes. Find and kill the monsters before they caused harm to anyone else. And find the man in the black coat before he could disappear again. It was from him that she would learn the most valuable lessons concerning the monsters.

She now had a concrete purpose. Feeling better than she had since the first night she'd discovered that evil was running rampant in her city, she rose and made ready to make her first contact with the mistresses of the Voyeurs website. Through a vague email, would these ladies realize what she'd really been up to the past several nights?

It would be interesting as hell to find out.

Chapter Four

"Are you sure it was the same woman?"

Edge gritted his teeth and answered once again. "I'm positive. It was she."

The Traveler turned and regarded The Elder from the shadows of his cowl. An unspoken message seemed to pass between them and Edge was hard-pressed not to ask to be let in on their secret conversation.

"What was she doing there, I wonder?" Tryton murmured, as if to himself.

Edge took a deep breath, knowing he was about to open up a Pandora's box that might haunt him for the rest of his days. "She was hunting the monsters. And doing a fair job of destroying them outnumbered and alone as she was when I came upon her."

"Another human warrior? It seems I've greatly underestimated the courage of humans of late. And their prowess in battle."

"What shall we do about her?" Edge asked the question even as he hoped for and dreaded the answer he felt sure would come from his leader. He didn't have long to wait.

"Perhaps she can be recruited, as Cady was. But only if she has the talents that will help us, of course. And only if the Council will allow it. She is, after all, still human," Tryton said. "What did you think of her, Edge? What were your first impressions of this human woman?"

That she had the eyes of a goddess, the body of a nymph and the voice of a siren...but these things he wouldn't share with Tryton. That she had the tightest, hottest, wettest sex he'd ever known seemed an inappropriate answer as well. But it was nonetheless true and it was all Edge had been able to think about since he'd left her in her home as the morning had dawned around them. She'd been beautiful in her exhaustion. Fragile. Sexy.

By the Horde, his balls ached and tightened just thinking about her.

He recalled the questions at hand and strove to keep his libido under tighter control. "She seems to have learned on her own to take the Daemons' hearts and to burn the evidence they leave behind. That tells me she is by no means dull-witted. And after having spoken with her, I've discovered that she deliberately pursues the Daemons. This tells me that she does not lack honor. Or courage. Perhaps she has Hunter Caste skills, as Cady did."

"You spoke with her?" The Traveler asked quietly.

"Yes, but only briefly." That was true enough, in a literal sense.

Again the two exchanged looks. Edge clenched his fists but held his silence.

"You may leave us now, Edge. Thank you for the news. I will no doubt have further instructions for your patrol tonight."

Edge bowed respectfully and left Tryton's antechamber, wondering what The Traveler and Tryton would discuss after he left them. Wondering if he'd just sealed the human woman's fate...or his own.

* * * * *

"Keep an eye on the Territories of Earth tonight, Grimm. And keep close to Edge. He will no doubt be looking for the human woman as doggedly as he will be looking for signs of the Horde."

"No doubt."

"I'd like to speak with her. Take her measure. Though first I will have to speak with our Watchers. I mean the Voyeurs." Tryton rolled his eyes and then smiled. "I still can't believe Steffy has them calling themselves by that ridiculous moniker. I hear they've actually received word from this human woman on their own end."

"It will be as you wish."

Tryton smiled. "I have every faith that it will." Arrogance fairly dripped from him. It was the ancient warrior's well-earned right.

"There is one thing," Grimm was moved to add.

"What is that?"

"I have a strange feeling about the human woman. You will have to tread carefully with her. All is not as is seems. I fear she is not like Cady or Steffy, even if she is a human and, as such, their kin."

"Grimm, you have ever been as useful as an oracle in our greatest times of need. I trust in your judgment...but I will meet her. And I will try to recruit her. Our ranks need this new blood, this human blood she brings. It has ever been so, though I've been too stubborn to welcome the addition in the past. You, more than anyone, know this."

Grimm was silent in the face of Tryton's will.

"As I said, try to meet her. Try to ascertain what it is about her that cautions you so. I'll learn what I can from Desondra and her group. But I still want you to arrange a meeting between she and I so that I, too, can study her. Perhaps it is nothing."

"Perhaps. You may be right," Grimm agreed, but in his thoughts he already knew differently.

Chapter Five

Emily rubbed her mucky hands negligently against the seat of her jeans. Killing monsters was dirty, smelly, tiresome business. No matter how hard she tried, she always seemed to ruin her clothing, and pretty soon she'd have to go out and buy more jeans and T-shirts for the task. Of course she'd purchase everything in dark colors this time to hide the stains of violence more easily.

One thing was preying on her mind more and more often now as each night came to a close. Pretty soon she'd have to return to her job. Much as she might wish it she couldn't afford to quit, but now that she had a nobler duty to perform each night she couldn't help wondering what to do about her police work. More and more she was beginning to lean towards the idea of switching to the day shift—the monsters were nocturnal after all—but that would stretch her thin as far as sleep was concerned. And forget having any kind of a social life, not that she had much of one in the first place.

Was she ready to sacrifice so much? Absolutely. But was she physically and mentally capable of keeping such a rigorous schedule? Emily wasn't too sure about that. What precious few hours of sleep she'd gotten had done much to recharge her, but there was no telling when next she would be able to sleep so long or so deeply again.

Insomnia was a fickle and tricky bedfellow and by no means could she count on banishing it from her life simply because she wanted it gone. If that were the case she'd have been free of sleepless nights — or days as the case may be — many years before this.

But she couldn't, in good conscience, give up this new fight she'd become embroiled in. To do so would smack too closely of cowardice or negligence for her liking. And if she turned her back on the horrible acts these beasts seemed intent on committing she'd be no better than they and no less evil. So the only answer seemed to be switching to the day shift. Perhaps even taking up a desk position within the department in order to keep her nights free for this more dangerous work.

Emily wandered the streets, searching for any signs of her quarry. She'd only killed two tonight, a far sight fewer than normal. But it was early yet, barely an hour past midnight and she had high hopes of finding and destroying more before her tour of duty was done.

There came the fall of footsteps behind her and she whirled about, raising her shotgun up before her as she did so. Luckily for the man in the black coat, she was able to stay her finger from pressing too tightly on the trigger before she recognized him in the murky darkness.

"You shouldn't sneak up on people like that. Especially people who might shoot first and ask questions later."

"I didn't sneak. I stepped heavily enough for you to hear me. You should be happy for that much of a warning from me."

"You're too cocky by far." She rolled her eyes.

The man in the black coat stepped closer, stalking her. "You're awfully brave behind the barrel of that gun. Shall I show you again how ineffectual that weapon is against me?"

Emily lowered the gun, but otherwise ignored his goading words. "You owe me for that, by the way. These things aren't cheap, I'll have you know. And a police officer's salary can only be stretched so far these days."

"Humans are so strange with their worship of green pieces of paper. There are more important things in life than money, let me assure you of that."

Emily snorted. "Be that as it may, money makes the world go 'round and I have too precious little of it to ignore the loss of a fine weapon."

"Perhaps I should pay you…after all, you deserve something after last night's performance. I'm not so callous as to forget it so quickly."

Emily felt as if he'd struck her. "W-what?" She felt her eyes widen in shock.

"I assume, like most humans, you require some compensation for allowing me such free access to your person. I suppose I owe you for that, as well as for the weapon." He sounded so flippant, so cool.

She swallowed hard. "Are you…are you calling me a whore?" It took every ounce of willpower she possessed not to shout the words at him.

"I am merely calling you human. Don't worry, I understand how it is with your kind." He reached into the pocket of his coat and removed an alarmingly thick wad of bills. "Would this be enough, do you think?"

Her finger twitched, moved towards the trigger of her gun once more. The man's eyes flashed down, catching the telltale angry movement. "You…you—" she paused and took a deep breath. She needed to calm down or else she'd lose every last shred of dignity that she possessed. "You can go to hell," she finished.

He held out the bills for her with long, elegant fingers. "Double this then, when next we meet. You were worth it, of course."

She reached out and roughly jerked the money from him, wadded it in her fist, and threw it back in his face. "Fuck. You."

"You already did that." He goaded her mercilessly, his mouth set in a hard line, his eyes cruel flames burning out at her from the shadows of his face.

Emily wanted to remain calm, to let him think she wasn't hurt or offended by his cruel words. But her temper—always explosive when stoked—got the better of her. She threw her gun at him. He fended it off too easily. She launched herself at him with a howl of rage.

He blocked her first two punches. And avoided her first well-aimed kick to the groin. It was too easy for him, with his incredible speed. However, the very apparent futility of her struggles only served to enrage her further and she threw her weight against him, tackling him to the ground.

He grunted.

She grinned a feral, triumphant grin, and jabbed her knee into his stomach. He jerked but did not cry out. Her grin faded and she growled. He rolled them over, assuming the dominant position over her, attempting to hold her to the ground with his hands at her wrists and his body straddling her.

Wriggling like an eel, she dislodged him enough to pull away, crawling on her hands and knees now like an awkward infant as he held on. His arms wrapped around her legs, bringing her to the ground again. He covered her back, trying to hold her still. She went limp.

But she was not defeated. Not by any means.

Waiting until he was just behind her, she flew up, butting his face with the back of her head. He grunted in pain and released her, grabbing his face. She scrambled away and gained her feet, only to return now that she had the advantage of height over him. She kicked out with her booted foot, catching him in the chest. He went down like a ton of bricks.

Smiling—more a wicked flash of her tightly clenched teeth than any real smile—she circled him as he rolled on the ground in an attempt to regain his feet.

Feeling no remorse, she kicked him in the stomach. Quick as a serpent, he caught her ankle, and twisted with brutal force. She twirled in the air and landed with a horrible thud on her back. The wind was knocked from her, but still she struggled. She was far too enraged not to.

Rolling awkwardly onto her side, she kicked him repeatedly in the shin. He grunted and grabbed his leg, but only managed in getting his fingers crushed under her kicking feet in doing so. She then managed to maneuver herself just so and began kicking out for his stomach and chest.

"Stop! Damn it, woman, stop it!" he shouted.

"No!" she screamed and continued her pummeling.

Suddenly, quick as a blink, he was on her. His body slammed down on hers brutally, scraping and cutting her back on the littered ground. "I don't want to hurt you," he gritted out, his face a mere breath away from her.

"Well I do want to hurt you," she spat up at him.

"I think you broke one of my ribs," he murmured, sounding oddly detached from the pain if his words were true. "Does that please your offended pride enough?"

"I wish I had broken them all—as well as that conceited head of yours."

He laughed, but it was a dark and self-depreciating noise, without humor or joy.

She didn't care for it. She roared and tried to buck him off of her.

"I'm sorry, Emily. I'm sorry for insulting you. It was wrong of me. I didn't mean it." He had to yell to be heard over her cries of impotent rage, holding her down with nearly bruising force.

"Sorry is not good enough."

"Sorry is all I have to give."

"I'll have your blood! I'm not a whore."

"I know." His voice softened to a beautiful, masculine timbre that would have lulled her and soothed her had she not been so completely enraged. "I know you're not a whore." His hands gentled upon her. He stroked her shoulders coaxingly.

"I wasn't myself," she cried out defensively, feeling the sting of tears with a sense of something akin to panic or shame.

He shushed her. "I believe you. And I am sorry. I was angry. I'm such an ass." He lowered his forehead to hers and breathed gently against her mouth. She couldn't help but notice how sweet and warm his breath was. His long lashes shielded his eyes from hers as he lowered them. "I can't tell you how sorry I am. My temper. It gets the better of me when you're near."

"Why? What did I ever do to you?"

You made me want you. Made me want you more than I've ever wanted another woman—human or Shikar.

But he would not tell her that. "Nothing. You've nothing to be ashamed of. I do. Please forgive me."

"No," she bit out.

"In time you'll have to."

"Bullshit. I don't have to do anything I don't want to. And I don't want to have anything more to do with you."

"If we'll be working together—which I've no doubt will be the case—you'll have to get over your anger. We can't be enemies, you and I."

"You made me your enemy."

"I know. I am ashamed of my lack of good grace." It had been too easy for him, really, to make her despise him. But now he wished to recall his goading words. He'd known too well how to insult her. How to debase her. He cursed himself for a thousand fools. "This was entirely my fault, I admit. Again, I am sorry."

Emily eased beneath him, turned her face away from his. "Let me up," she said softly.

"Will you talk with me?"

"Let me up…and I'll consider it."

He rose in an alien, fluid movement, his body moving as if invisible strings pulled it into motion or as if human physicality had no effect on how his muscles worked. He took her hand and gently helped her to her feet. She jerked her hand away from his as soon as she could manage it.

"I have a proposition for you," he said.

"Kiss my ass. That first time between us was the last," she swore.

He smiled, but felt goaded by her vow just the same. Last time indeed. Perhaps…and perhaps not. A few moments ago he wanted nothing more than to push her away — to keep her from getting further under is skin. But now all he could think about was how beautiful and fragile she looked, flushed and disheveled from their struggle.

And she'd bruised him. He'd not lied in telling her she may have broken one of his ribs. For some reason he couldn't fathom, her show of strength was serving as a sort of aphrodisiac to him. It turned him on mightily to know that she could hold her own in battle with him. He wondered what it would be like to wrestle naked with her. He almost came right then and there with the images that erotic thought evoked.

His near loss of control shamed him.

"It's not that kind of proposition." He managed to bring his mind back to the matter at hand. "I have a friend who wishes to meet you. Who wishes to ask you a few questions about what you've been doing out here these past several nights."

"Why should I care to meet any friend of yours?"

"Because you seek answers too, no doubt. And Tryton can give you all the answers you could ever ask for."

"Tryton, huh? What an odd name. And how about yours? What's your name?'

"Edge."

"Well I'm sorry I can't say it was nice to meet you, Edge. And now I really must be going. I'll thank you to stay out of my way. Or I may just shoot you the next time I see you."

He ignored her words for the most part, though oddly enough his heart still hurt to hear the venom spill from her lips. "You aren't the least bit curious about what's going on around you? You would give up this chance to learn?"

Emily sighed wearily. She wasn't so stubborn that she couldn't admit to a little curiosity, if only to herself. "Where is this friend of yours?"

"Waiting for you."

"That didn't answer my question. Where is he waiting?"

"Somewhere safe. Underground and far away from humans. Near the Earth's core, if you want specifics." Why he was being so upfront with her he couldn't have said. Normally they kept their secrets until the last when it came to sharing with humans. How odd that he felt this overwhelming need to be completely honest with her now.

"Impossible," she barked out, waving his words away. She'd been a fool to continue this conversation anyway.

"Very possible, and I can arrange a meeting tonight if you wish."

"My ass. Go sell your lies to someone who's buying. I'm off." She turned to go.

"You've seen some pretty fantastic things over the past several days. You would balk at believing in this small thing?"

"A guy named Tryton—as in the sea god—is waiting to meet me near the Earth's core."

"Yes."

"That doesn't sound a little far-fetched to you?"

"It is the truth, human." He sounded decidedly impatient now.

"That's crazy. There's no way that can be possible. The Earth's core? Come on."

"You are quite the cynical one, considering that you are covered in the blood of beasts, and standing before a man who can shoot blades out of his body."

She had to give him that one. "Fine." Emily tried to imagine what she might be getting herself into, and realized it was probably best to leave her imagination out of the whole affair. "Take me to meet this friend of yours —"

A dozen monsters came out of the night, heading straight for Edge with teeth and claws bared. They gave no warning. As sudden as a thought they were upon them, growling in their foul tongue, like beasts in a feral rage. There was no escape for the two warriors, no time to formulate a defense. Too quickly they were cornered in the alleyway. They were surrounded by their enemies, with no choice but to fight, highly outnumbered though they were.

Emily gasped and darted for her discarded weapon, which was thankfully, miraculously close enough for her to reach. She jerked the shotgun up before her, only to have it knocked painfully from her grasp by one of the beasts as it reached them. Edge struck out with such amazing speed and grace that Emily barely had time to register his movements as she tried to palm another weapon. Five-foot blades — swords of glowing blue and white — appeared in his hands and he swung them with deadly precision at their enemies. The monster that had struck out at her fell first, crumbling to little pieces at her feet.

Heads rolled, bodies fell, but still more monsters came to take the place of the fallen, appearing out of the shadows like nightmare visions. Emily's hand wrapped around the grip of a handgun and she fired it, point blank, into the hellish face of the closest monster. It fell back and without wasting time to revel in her small victory, she turned and fired into another, and another, until she was forced to reload.

There were just too many of them to gain an immediate foothold against their bombardment.

Emily had never seen so many at once. And though she had suspected from the first that these vile creatures had been holding back from harming her, she was shocked to see just how very deadly they could be when they wished to destroy their prey. These beasts hated Edge. They feared him. And though they still only sought to disarm her — or so it seemed — they fought with a terrible purpose to wound and destroy him utterly.

They were cruel and vicious. Their growls were full of hate and fear of the warrior. But Edge was a magician with his blades, cutting his enemies down with such ease that Emily found herself envious of his brilliant skill. She would give anything — anything at all — to be able to fight like him.

He was as deadly as the monsters. Deadlier. But with the force of good behind each of his deathblows he had a power that was unequaled even in the sum total of the evil that surrounded them. The creatures didn't stand a chance against him.

The monsters seemed to realize this fact after at least half their number had fallen under the blades. To Emily's amazement they turned their attentions to her.

"Emily." The monster was reaching out for her, its intent unclear, and Emily hurried to reload her weapon. "Come."

"Kiss my ass," she growled and emptied her clip into the monster with unsteady hands. To hear her name on the lips of that creature...it was a horror she felt would be best to forget. As quickly as possible.

Though Edge struck down monster after monster, it seemed there was an endless supply of them appearing from the shadows. He grabbed her arm with one hand, cut apart an enemy with the other, and shouted above the din. "If we can manage it, we have to get out of here. Fast."

That was the understatement of a century. The night was swarming with their foes. They were vastly outnumbered. Retreat was imperative, but even so, Emily was hard-pressed to give up the fight. After a few more seconds, and a few more fallen bodies, she relented.

"Do you have any of those little vials with you?" she asked him in a near roar. The sounds of battle were deafening, the cries of the monsters earsplitting.

"Here." He shoved a fistful of them at her unquestioningly, using his other hand to fend off one of the beasts. His movements were so swift Emily could barely see them beyond a blur.

Emily steeled herself. "Get ready to run," she called and in the next breath she flung the vials onto the asphalt. The glass shattered and the contents roared into flame. Wasting no time Emily raced towards the fire even as the monsters stepped back in their fear of it, clearing a path as they did so.

She didn't have to glance behind her to know that Edge was following swiftly upon her heels. His presence was palpable behind her as she fled, ducking from one alleyway to the next, going deeper into dregs of the city in the hopes that their enemies would get lost in the maze.

After putting a good mile between them and the battle scene behind them, Emily grew tired and slowed her flight.

"I think we lost them," she said, hoping it was so.

A shadow passed before them. Two hands reached out of the dark. Emily's head swam dizzily...and the dark city around her disappeared.

Chapter Six

"If you ever surprise me like that again, Traveler, I will spin you on the tip of a Foil until you beg for mercy. If I didn't respect you as one of Tryton's closest confidants, I would do it right now anyway."

"I'd like to see you try it." The Traveler's voice was so darkly compelling, so completely unlike any other voice Emily had ever heard that she was almost mesmerized by it. Though his words were threatening, she could hear a hint of a smile beneath them. It was odd, this touch of humor, coming from a man whose power seemed to roll off of him in tangible, frightening waves.

"What just happened?" she asked, trembling. She looked around them, at the great stone cavern that dwarfed them. "Where the hell are we?"

"This is our world, Emily. The world of the Shikar," a new voice informed her.

She turned and saw a tall man with long, pale blond hair approach them. "That doesn't answer either of my questions, you know," she pointed out.

"All in due time. Worry about it no more. I am Tryton." He bowed to her, a courtly show of respect, before turning to the two men who silently watched.

"Thank you for keeping her safe, Edge. Though from what I understand Emily has held her own quite well." The man—Tryton—winked at her. "The Traveler was acting on my command when he brought you here. Do not be troubled by it further."

Edge bowed, his gesture one of utmost respect.

Who is this guy, Emily wondered, that even Edge is deferential to him?

"Though, I think it was a little dramatic an effort on your part, Traveler. Don't you?" Tryton spoke to the exceedingly tall man hidden in the folds of a deep cowl and cloak.

"As you say, Elder." The man's voice held all the secrets of the world, even as it remained lightly tinged with humor. Emily shuddered delicately to hear him speak and wasn't sure if she was frightened or intrigued by this strange fellow.

"Please leave us, so that we may become better acquainted," he implored the two men and seconds later Emily and Tryton were alone in the stone chamber.

The man turned to her, regarding her for a long silent moment with his clear yellow eyes. "Please. Have a seat." He motioned to a placement of heavily cushioned chairs behind her. They were situated before a great fireplace which Emily only noticed after Tryton's gesture.

So the room wasn't merely a huge cave as she may have thought, but an incredible anteroom, sporting all the fashions a rich feudal lord might have required. "Why have you brought me here?" she asked with great curiosity.

"I wanted to meet you," he replied simply.

"Why not just come and knock on my door? It's obvious you know quite a lot about me—I'm sure you could easily get my address. If not from Edge then from wherever else you get your information. Why all the fuss?"

Tryton took a seat in the chair opposite her. He was so tall that even sitting, Emily had to tilt her head back to meet his eyes. He sighed before answering and it was a weary sound. Beyond weary. "I do not venture to the surface very often anymore. It has been many years since I left this place, actually. It is far easier for me to have you brought before me this way. I hope I haven't given you a poor impression...?"

"Well it's more than obvious to me that you're all a bunch of arrogant people. It only took me a couple of encounters with you guys to figure that out, but if it's a poor impression, at least it's a lasting one." She smiled when she said it to soften the words, not truly intending to offend him.

Tryton laughed. "It certainly doesn't help that you've met two of our most arrogant warriors, either. But high-handed or not, we are honorable. No harm will come to you here."

"Thanks for the reassurance, but I can hold my own just fine — as you said."

"Yes. There is that. Then I shall get right to the point. Tell me, Emily. Why is it we've suddenly found you, a human, fighting these Daemons?"

Emily frowned and asked one of her own questions instead. "You know they're called Daemons? I thought it was just those college kids on that website who called them that because they thought Latin was so cool a language to borrow from."

"You mean the Voyeurs?" He smiled when Emily started. "I know about them of course, don't look so surprised. But no—that website's information is deliberately vague at times, as you'll learn soon enough—it isn't only because of the Latin that these beings are named thus. We call them Daemons, in part, because the name of their leader is Daemon. Ancient peoples of your world, when Latin was yet a young language, named this being Daemonio when he nearly broke the world, and the name has stuck over time." His eyes clouded and Emily wondered at the secrets he hid there behind them. He seemed ill inclined to elaborate on it, but continued after only a short pause.

"There is no other more appropriate name that we have for these devils—all of them Daemon's creation. Daemon, monster, devil. They are a part of a most terrible and evil army—the Daemon Horde. Their sole purpose is to feed their endless appetites for psychic energy through the consumption of human flesh and blood. Or Shikar, if they can actually catch one of us."

"I've seen them eat." She shuddered. "You're saying they get some kind of sick, weird battery power from feeding on the living?"

"Yes. That's it exactly." He seemed pleased that she'd grasped the situation so quickly. "Any human will do, for all humans possess some small amounts of this 'battery power.' But they thrive on the truly gifted, those humans who are psychic."

"There's no such thing as a psychic." She scoffed at the idea.

"Oh but you're wrong. And I've no doubt that you possess these very gifts, which make you so valuable to the Horde. Else why would they be so keen on hunting you?"

"I hate to tell you this, but I don't think they're after me to eat me," she said with a small frown.

Tryton seemed to start, though his expression never changed. "Why would you think that? They've been after you for many nights now, this I've been told —"

"That's debatable as I've been hunting them too," she interjected. "But suppose, for the sake of argument, that they were hunting me? Even so, they haven't succeeded in hurting me yet. They don't seem to want to hurt me. Not really. So it makes for easier kills on my part. I think you're wrong about their intent."

Tryton smiled, looking a little relieved, as if he saw through the enigma she had presented before him with her words. "Perhaps you are underestimating your skills as a warrior a little too much? You must indeed be a formidable foe if you can call the Daemons easy kills."

"No. I'm no wuss," she quickly amended, her ego needing that small appeasement, "but they don't fight me the same way they fight Edge. I saw them. When they fight him they're vicious and nearly unstoppable. If they came at me with such deadly intent there isn't much chance I could get away from them unscathed. They're holding back from me."

"How can this be?" Tryton asked, looking incredulous. It was an expression that Emily instinctively sensed he didn't wear often. "I don't understand."

"I don't either. But then I understand practically nil of what's been going on around me for the past several days. I've just been sort of rolling with the punches, so to speak."

"You must be mistaken, Emily. The Daemons would not so doggedly hunt a human without the hunger for the kill uppermost in their minds."

"Well I'm sorry, but the facts are the facts," she emphasized. "The only thing I know for any certainty is that these things want me to go with them somewhere—"

"What? What did you say? How can you know that?" Tryton fired at her.

Emily bristled under his burning gaze, uncomfortable with his volatility and feeling her own temper rise at his ruthless questioning. "They know my name. They keep saying 'Emily. Come. Emily, come.' Like that, only a helluva lot more scary." She tried and failed to mimic the Daemons' awful words. She shuddered from the memory. However safe she might be at the moment, such a thing very nearly terrified her. "They don't want to kill me, at least not right away. I'm sure of it. I assume they want to take me somewhere first. Why, I don't know. Hell, I don't even care. I just want to get rid of the bastards, the sooner the better, while keeping myself out of their claws."

Tryton rose from his chair so swiftly that Emily's eyes were unable to follow the movement clearly. Grabbing a fistful of powder from an urn on the mantle, he threw it into the fire and said something unintelligible to her ears.

"What are you doing?"

"This is *fl'shan* sand. I use it to call any of my people to me. Like a telepathic pager, or so Steffy would say. As it is made from the saliva of Incinerators it can also be used as an incendiary." His mind was clearly not on the subject and he seemed only to explain it to her out of common courtesy.

"Who the hell is Steffy?" She was moved to ask the one question when she had countless others that were no doubt more relevant, but Tryton's attention was already diverted.

The man in the hooded cloak appeared at Tryton's side and Emily jumped in her seat, surprised. Though she'd seen the Daemons blip in and out like magic before her very eyes, she'd yet to see it done with such a quietly swift finesse as this man managed to employ.

So that was how she'd gotten here. This man had taken her and Edge with him. Somehow. "Cool," she breathed in surprised awe.

Tryton moved to her side, towering over her. "Tell him what you just told me."

"Why? What's going on?" she asked, very unsettled by his intensity.

Tryton was too impatient to wait for her to do as he asked, nor did he answer her questions. He turned to the shadowy man—The Traveler—and spat out in a near rage, "The Daemons know her. They know her name! How do they know her name? And why would they even care to?"

The cowl moved as the man cocked his head and Emily saw the indistinct blur of his features. He was a lovely man; of that there could be no doubt. She wondered if any of these Shikars were ugly because thus far, from all she'd seen of them they seemed to be a race of truly beautiful men.

"I cannot say," he answered softly.

"They speak to her, call her name and tell her to come with them. What in the name of all that is sacred could they possibly want with a hostage? For that is all I can assume the Daemons wish for when they implore her to join them."

The Traveler was silent for a long, tense moment. "It is as I feared then. She is not psychic, Tryton. I felt this truth from the first. I tried to warn you of my doubts. She is powerful in her own way, but not in the way most useful to the Horde."

"How can this be?" Tryton roared. "And why do they want her?"

"I cannot say. I fear they have an agenda all their own. But for a certainty, if she were truly powerful they would have fed on her already despite any plans they might have to the contrary. They have not the strength to deny their appetites for long."

"Hey!" Emily interjected. "I'm still here, remember? Why not ask me what I think?"

"You're a human, Emily. You cannot understand what we are about here, not yet."

"Did you mean for that to be insulting? Because I am very insulted." She rose from her seat, squaring her shoulders. "I may be human. I may be new to all of this. But I am not inferior and if you're going to stand around discussing something that concerns me, I will be a part of the conversation. Is that clear?" she bit out savagely.

Tryton was taken aback by her words. His eyes widened and he appeared dumbfounded for several seconds. He rallied, schooled his features once more into his serene, polite mask, and cleared his throat. "You are right. I apologize for my rudeness, Emily. I am not myself. I find I am beyond surprised and confused by this information you have divulged."

"Why?" She nearly yelled it, in the midst of her growing agitation.

"Because the Daemons are not normally cunning enough to discover the identity of their prey. And why should they want to? They have ever been mindless, animated only by their most basic and elementary hungers," The Traveler answered her. "We are surprised that they know you. Surprised that they spoke to you. Surprised that they have held to some secret agenda in seeking to capture you...without feeding on you."

"But what could they want with her?" Tryton asked.

"I don't know."

"Retrieve Obsidian and Cady. Have them assemble their team before nightfall on the morrow. Do it now," Tryton commanded.

The Traveler disappeared immediately.

Tryton turned to Emily once more. "Would you be willing to help aid our fight against these creatures, Emily? Would you put yourself at risk, allow us to use you as bait to lure these creatures, so that we can discover their new purpose?"

Emily looked him in the eye, judging him and finding him an admirable sort. Obviously his own people respected and held him in high regard. She could do no less, though she barely knew him. Something about him compelled her to trust in him, to revere him. So it was that the choice became blessedly clear to her. With barely a hesitation Emily took the step she now realized she'd been planning to take all along. Only Tryton had given her the upper hand in asking her to aid them, though he couldn't have known it, surely. "On one condition. And one condition only," she said at last.

"What is that?" Tryton asked.

"You let me be a part of all this. When the time comes that I've met my end of the bargain and let you use me to lure these things to you…you let me join your people in this fight."

"Be careful you know for certain what you ask of me," he warned.

"Those are my terms. I want to be a part of this fight. I want to work with you to keep my people safe. That's what you do isn't it? Protect people like me from these things? That's why Edge is always out there at night, fighting the Daemons."

"Yes. You have it aright. Though it is not so noble as it may sound. We want these creatures stamped out utterly, from our world, from yours, from all planes of existence."

"So you want these creatures dead. I want them gone from my city. Dead or otherwise, I don't really care about the particulars. Let me learn from you, let me fight with you, and we may reach that goal together."

"But to let you join us…I would have to ask that you leave your normal life behind. Becoming a warrior, a member of our army, will consume all of your time. It will become your life, one you can never turn your back on. You cannot take half measures, and we cannot risk discovery by letting you roam as you will." Tryton's gaze roved over her, as if taking her measure.

"Where will I live? How will I survive?"

"You will be a part of our family. You will not be the first human we have taken into our ranks. We always take care of our own. You will live here. You will want for nothing. But you will fight…and you may die."

The risks were great, but she found that she didn't care. Her course was plotted, her heart and courage were set upon the path before her and she would not falter. "Fine. So long as you promise me I can help to make a difference, help to protect my people, I'll leave my life behind as you ask. I'll make a life here, with your people. And you will treat me as one of your own." The opportunity was more than she'd dared to hope for. It was a perfect solution to her dilemma, and though she'd be giving up her life, she found that it was not too great a sacrifice for the new life he now offered her... She stilled. It was too perfect.

Her eyes met Tryton's, saw the trace of smug triumph in their fiery depths. Had he planned this from the start? Planned to have her join them? Is that why he'd wished to meet her all along? She glimpsed the small twitching curve of his lips, saw him ease the smile away with haste and secrecy. The devil had schemed all this from the very beginning.

And she thought she'd been so clever, that she'd had the upper hand in this odd negotiation between them. She wondered, looking now into Tryton's too astute gaze, just how he'd known to maneuver her so easily. For maneuver her he had, no doubt, and she'd realized it too late.

She smiled, seeing in him many of the qualities she'd always respected and admired in a leader. He was cunning, this one. But he was kind as well. Somehow she knew it. To trust in him was not completely foolhardy, no matter his hidden machinations.

Tryton smiled back, and had she but known it, she would have been surprised that his thoughts were not too dissimilar from hers.

"Agreed," he said.

"Goody." Emily felt as if a new journey lie ahead of her...and wondered with no small amount of apprehension if perhaps she might all too soon find herself in far over her head.

"Let me show you to your new living quarters. I will have all of your belongings transported to your new home immediately, so that you can grow more comfortable here the soonest."

"What about my job? My apartment? I'll need to settle my affairs so that no one misses me."

"Do you have family? Friends? People who would grieve if you disappeared from their lives?"

It chagrined her to note that there was no one who would truly care. She had no family, not anymore, and no close friendships with anyone.

Tryton knew her answer having seen the frown upon her face. "Don't worry about it. We'll take care of everything. There will be no searches for you, no missing person bulletins over which to feel guilt. For now, rest. No doubt you need sleep before we indulge in further discussion."

It was hard to put her trust and faith in this man, who was virtually a stranger. But she realized that to balk now would gain her no advantage. She would let him do as he promised and take care of the affairs of her former life. For now, she was tired, so very tired. She nodded her assent to his words. Tryton reached out, surprising her, and laid a gentle yet bracing hand upon her shoulder.

"Tomorrow night will begin your new life with us. In time, all your fears and questions will be laid to rest, I assure you. Welcome to the Shikar Alliance, Emily."

Chapter Seven

Emily's eyes darted open in the darkness. Something, some sound or movement, had awakened her. Her surroundings were strange, alien to her, so it took several long moments for her to get her bearings there in her large, exquisitely soft Shikar bed. Tryton had been as good as his word, and already all of her worldly belongings surrounded her, giving her some small comfort in this new home of hers. She was grateful to him for that. Though it seemed as black as midnight, she sensed it was no later than midday on the surface of her world—and her alarm clock stated as much in glowing red numbers on the bedside table.

"I did not mean to startle you." That voice was a brush of thick velvet against her mind.

"What are you doing here, Traveler?" Feeling no small amount of skittishness at his unexpected—uninvited—presence, she masked her unease with the grumpy words.

"Do not fear me." His voice was nearly a whisper, barely a murmur.

Emily sat up in the bed, instinctively pulling the covers to her throat to cover her nudity, wondering how well he could see her in the dark. "I'm not afraid of you." It was only a small lie.

"Good." There was the hint of a smile in his quiet voice. His hand came out, disembodied in the darkness, and touched her hair with a light caress.

Emily pulled back uneasily.

"Sorry." He immediately withdrew his hand. "I couldn't help myself. It has been so long since I touched a human like this. In gentle comfort, instead of necessity."

"Back off, buddy." She felt his latent sensuality spill out over her like a warm, inviting blanket.

He chuckled softly. "I meant no insult. I do not desire you as a man desires a woman, though you are beautiful. Have no fear on that score. You intrigue me, that is all. Your fragile humanity and iron strength of will intrigue me. It reminds me of someone I knew, briefly, some time ago."

Emily didn't know whether or not she was insulted or relieved by his words. "I'm not fragile." It was all she could think to say in response.

Again he laughed. "No, I suppose not. You are here with us, after all, and The Elder would never have invited you otherwise." He moved in the darkness. Emily felt his shifting, but it was still too dark for her to see him.

It was too black. Not the normal dimness of night, but preternaturally dense. The Traveler, Emily guessed, was the cause of the darkness. He was hiding himself in the blackness, using it as a shield between them. What an odd race of beings she'd allied herself with.

"What are you doing here?" she asked him again.

"I just wanted to check in on you."

"Why?" She was bewildered.

"I do not know why." That black magic voice sounded much aggrieved, as if he truly didn't understand his own motives. "But I feel as if I should look out for you. You have not the added advantage of psychic power that the others do. It makes you vulnerable."

"I can take care of myself." She rolled her eyes. Did all Shikars think humans weak and helpless?

"I know. I know you can," he murmured. "But I needed to reassure myself."

"You are so weird."

He chuckled ruefully. "Perhaps."

"You said I remind you of someone." She prodded him to continue.

"Yes. You do." His voice was growing more and more faint, as if he were moving far away from her. Far, far away.

"Who?" she asked, raising her voice for him to hear her across what felt like a swiftly growing distance between them.

"A woman I knew once. She died. I could not save her...but perhaps I can save you."

As silently as he'd come, he left her with those words in the darkness of her room. What had he meant by that? She couldn't begin to guess.

It was a long, long while before Emily fell asleep again.

* * * * *

"Wow. I'd kill to have a body like yours, Emily."

"You make me sick, Steffy. As if you have any room to complain—at least your hips aren't as wide as a barn like mine are."

"Actually I'd love wider hips. I look too much like a boy as I am. I'd love a few curves here and there."

Cady snorted.

Steffy harrumphed.

Emily tried not to laugh at the by-play between the two friends. She didn't know them very well—they may not take kindly to her laughter. And it seemed inappropriate for the moment. Here she was, standing naked before two virtual strangers, who were preparing to paint her with some kind of liquid body armor.

"You're going to have to shave that bush," Cady said, pointing to Emily's pubic hair. "This stuff hurts like hell when you pull it away from body hair. For now, I guess you can put some panties on underneath it. It won't be as pretty but..."

"I don't see why I have to wear this. Liquid latex isn't as much protection as a Kevlar vest."

"It's not liquid latex," Steffy said adamantly. "It's applied and removed like LL, but after that it's not similar at all. This stuff is awesome—Agate designed it. Well, I have to boast it was my idea that it should work like LL—for easy application and removal—but other than that this is Agate's creation. This armor is so strong, not even a bullet can get through it. It's made from the dung of Horde Canker-Worms—nearly impenetrable stuff when it's dry."

Emily knew better than to ask what Canker-Worms were and tried her best to ignore the disturbing word dung.

"Not that I'd suggest stepping in front of any bullets, even with this armor on," Cady quipped. "They bruise like hell." She grinned.

"But I've seen Edge cut through it like tissue paper." Emily's breath hitched at the memory of why he'd cut through it.

Cady and Steffy looked at each other and burst into laughter.

"Yeah. We heard all about that," Cady got out between guffaws.

"Heard about what?" Emily felt her cheeks heat with a blush.

"How you and Edge went at it like two teenagers in the back of an alley," Steffy said.

"You know about that?" She swallowed hard against her embarrassment, gritting her teeth. How could they know about that? Was nothing sacred to the Shikars? Was nothing secret? She donned her underwear and watched in trepidation as Cady advanced on her with a pot of the liquid armor and a thick paintbrush.

"Yeah. So. Was he any good?"

"Cady! Have some tact, girl." Steffy winked at Emily. "Well, was he any good?"

Emily laughed — she couldn't help it. "I'm not telling you anything. You'll just blab it."

"Don't worry that we'll tell Edge. We women keep our secrets amongst ourselves. Now tell all — leave nothing out."

"Yeah. Tell us everything." Steffy sat and watched as Cady applied the first strokes of 'paint' to Emily's outstretched arm.

"How did you find out?" Edge didn't seem the type to brag of his conquests to others.

"We have our ways." Cady whistled out the opening theme of The Twilight Zone. "Now spill the beans, chick."

"It was good, I guess." She laughed self-consciously. She'd never shared such secrets with other women, but these two were so friendly and genuinely infectious with their enthusiasm. She liked them already. "I'm not sure what you want to know."

"Everything," the two women said in unison, then laughed.

"He was..." She cleared her throat uncomfortably. "He was rough. But it was nice. Very nice."

"Shikars can be such rough and ready lovers. But they can be tender, too. If you want them to be." Steffy smiled dreamily.

"You only know that your Shikar lover is like that," Cady reminded her.

"Are you saying that Sid is always tender and soft with you?"

Cady blushed and her eyes glazed over. "No. You're right. Shikar men are rough—but they are soooo good when they're rough."

"Yes. I thought so, too, at the time." Emily chuckled at the two obviously love-struck women.

Steffy sobered. "At the time? But not now?"

Emily stiffened. She hadn't meant to reveal so much.

"What changed your mind?" Cady pressed, stroking the paintbrush over the last patch of exposed skin on Emily's forearm. A thick, black coat of the liquid armor enclosed her arm from shoulder to wrist.

"Nothing."

"No, no, no. You have to share now," Steffy prodded.

Cady was silent, studying her with those yellow-orange eyes of hers. Emily tried not to fidget under the Shikar woman's intense regard.

"Edge changed my mind."

"What did he do?"

"Well last night—the night after we were...you know." She faltered. Confiding was uncomfortable work. She'd never been able to do it with her sister or mother before their deaths. She wasn't sure she'd be able to now, with these women who were still virtually strangers to her.

"Go on," Steffy urged, bouncing with eagerness to hear more. "Don't clam up now."

"Last night he offered to pay me for my services. He practically called me a prostitute—and threw what we'd done together in my face."

"What a jerk!" Steffy gasped.

"What did you do?" Cady asked softly.

"I beat the snot out of him. Or I tried to, anyway," she admitted with a grin.

Her audience roared with laughter.

"I wish I could have seen his face. Edge is so stoic...I can't imagine him being laid low. And by a human woman. It must have really chafed him good."

"I wonder why he treated you that way?" Cady murmured. "He's usually so courteous—to a fault, even. I didn't know he could be so rude."

"His temper can be pretty nasty. Especially during training—he's a real drag sometimes. I've noticed, if he gets too mad, his mouth tends to runs away with a mind all its own. He can be pretty venomous sometimes," Steffy informed them. "Don't take it too hard Emily. Edge is just...edgy, I guess."

"Just when you think you know all there is to know about your teammates," Cady muttered.

"Did he apologize after you knocked some sense into him? Please say he did."

"Yeah. But that doesn't make it right," Emily defended.

"Why not?" Cady frowned. "Didn't you think he was sorry?"

"I guess so. But he shouldn't have said such horrible things. He tried to hand me a wad of money, for God's sake! How can I just let that go?"

Steffy laughed. "Girl, not that I blame you for being angry—you've every right—but you've got a lot to learn about men. Especially Shikar men."

"Yeah. They can be incredibly tactless sometimes. We women have to just let that go, or else the world would be a mess. Not a day goes by without Sid saying or doing something that just makes me want to wring his stubborn neck. But I have to get over it—or else kill him, which would really only make me sad once I'd gotten over my upset."

Emily gritted her teeth. Surely they weren't taking the sides of the men against her? She should have expected as much. They were Shikars after all and blood, as they say, was thicker than water. She kept silent and let them continue.

"Cinder's no better. Half of the time he thinks he being cute or funny, when he's really just being a total pain. But I love the guy—so I try to ignore his faults and forgive him when he gets too out of hand. After I make him do something he hates, of course. Like eat a hotdog—he can't stand those things—but all I do is tell him how much I miss my human food and he lets me take him out for his punishment." Steffy laughed wickedly.

"Wait. Your human food? I thought you were a Shikar?" Emily looked into Steffy's undeniably Shikar eyes, forgetting in her curiosity to give the two women the silent treatment.

"I am now. But I wasn't always."

"We both used to be human, just like you," Cady confirmed.

"I don't understand." Emily was stunned by her words.

"We were changed."

"How?"

Cady and Steffy exchanged meaningful glances. "Are you sure you want to know?" Cady asked, turning back to her.

"Yes. Tell me," Emily stressed.

"Well. It's going to sound really weird."

"Tell me."

"Our husbands changed us. Through unprotected sex. Their come is like a poison to humans. It can kill us."

"What?" Emily exclaimed.

"Let me explain, Cady. You're scaring her."

"I'm not scared," Emily said indignantly. She really wasn't. Was she?

"Look. It's like this," Steffy explained. "Shikar men, when they lay with a human, have to use a condom. They absolutely have to, because their semen can be deadly, if ingested in any way by their human partner. It will kill them—just like that." Steffy snapped her fingers for emphasis. "But with Cady and I, it was different—"

Cady interrupted. "All finished with your arms. Now your boobs. Suck in a deep breath so they're as full and perky as possible." She laughed.

"As I was saying." Steffy glared at Cady, who merely shrugged and began slathering paint all over Emily's chest. "Cady and I are different from most humans. We were psychic. And Tryton says that it's because of this that we didn't really die."

"I still don't understand," Emily admitted.

"You've met The Traveler?" Cady asked.

"Yes." She remembered the man's strange visit to her during the middle of the night and shivered.

Cady thankfully seemed oblivious to her reaction. "Well, when the time came that we were exposed to our husband's semen, The Traveler was there to keep us alive. He's like the Grim Reaper. He can travel back and forth between the realms of the living and the dead. So when we 'died,' he Traveled to the afterlife and kept us from going into the light that waited to take us—wherever. Heaven, Hell, I don't know."

"What does being psychic have to do with it, then? If The Traveler was the one who saved you?"

"Tryton's theory is that it's psychic power which helps to actually sustain the soul once it is returned to our bodies after our human death. Without that power, our soul would just go back to the other side, unfettered, and our bodies wouldn't have the strength to change into that of a Shikar."

"It is our psychic energy which fuels the change and locks our soul to our physical form," Cady clarified.

"That's messed up," Emily said incredulously.

"Yeah." Steffy laughed.

"But that still doesn't explain why you changed into a Shikar. Or does it?"

"Shikar semen is the catalyst. It causes the change, the change causes death, and when we're brought back the transformation is complete and we are no longer human," Steffy answered.

Emily thought it over, pensive.

"So. Why didn't you forgive Edge? Was he not a good enough lover to forgive?"

Emily sighed. It was obvious that Cady wasn't going to let the issue die a quiet death. "He was a good lover, I suppose. But I don't know him very well and…I think its best we just leave it at that one fling between us. Especially if we're going to be working together."

"What does working together have to do with anything?" Cady asked.

"Everything. I do not have relationships with my co-workers."

Cady rolled her eyes. "Co-workers. Sheesh. We're not on a job here. We're living. Things are different here than they are in the human world."

"Well whatever the case may be, I wasn't myself when Edge and I were together. I would never have done so foolish a thing if I'd been in my right mind. I didn't even know his name at the time!"

"What do you mean you weren't in your right mind?"

"I'm an insomniac. When Edge and I met, I hadn't slept for so many days I'd lost count. I was in hyper-reality mode. I wasn't thinking clearly at all."

"And now that you've had some sleep, you're not attracted to Edge anymore?" Steffy asked.

Emily had to be honest. "I wouldn't say that. He's very appealing. But he's not my type at all. He's so…arrogant. Stubborn. Cocky."

The two Shikar women laughed.

"Arrogant, stubborn, cocky men are the best mates for arrogant, stubborn, cocky women," Cady said in between chuckles.

"I'm not any of those things." Emily frowned.

They laughed again, clearly disbelieving in her words.

"I'm sorry to have to break it to you but if you weren't, Em, you wouldn't be here." Cady's paintbrush had finished with her front and was now moving to her back, starting at her shoulders. "Lift your hair."

Steffy grinned. "God, I love your hair, girl. Is it permed or natural?"

"Natural." Emily squirmed uncomfortably. She'd never been able to accept compliments with any real grace.

"My hair would probably just frizz if I cut it like yours." Cady shook the long, fat braid trailing down her back like a rope.

"It used to be shorter, about chin length. But it made me look so young."

"What's wrong with looking young?"

"Nothing. But my job is a hellluva lot easier if I look a littler older."

"Well amongst the Shikars you're not judged on age or looks. You're judged on your skills, your honor, and your loyalty." Steffy smiled.

"It sounds divine." Emily giggled as Cady painted the small of her back, tickling her. She blushed upon hearing that sound come from her own lips—she never giggled. Neither of the women seemed to notice her lapse, however, and she was grateful for that.

"It is." Steffy sighed. "You'll love it here. I just know it."

"You'll do well here, Emily. Don't worry about a thing. You're one of us now. Nothing else matters."

Chapter Eight

Emily smoothed her hands down over the jeans and T-shirt that covered the risqué liquid armor that was painted on her skin beneath them. "I don't see how this is going to protect me any better than my vest," she admitted.

"Trust me, it will," Steffy assured her.

"Well, we're all set. Sundown is in an hour or so. Tryton will want to brief us before we go above, no doubt. But before then I want you to come to the armory and pick out some weapons."

"Oh, the armory is so great, Emily! It's Cady's addition to the Shikar world, of course, and just about every weapon you could possibly imagine is in there."

"What's a girl to do without easy access to some guns?" Cady said with a deceptively elfin smile. "Getting a stocked armory was my first priority when I came here."

"Besides birthing your son, of course." Steffy smiled at her friend.

"You have a son?" For some reason Emily hadn't given much thought to the possibility of Shikar children. She certainly hadn't seen any.

"Oh yes. Armand." Cady's eyes took on the warmth that only a mother can have for her beloved offspring. "He's three years old now and already the spitting image of his father, heaven help me."

"How can you…?" She couldn't think of the best way to ask, so she said it bluntly. "How can you go off to fight if you have a child? Don't you worry about not coming back some night?"

Cady sobered and laid a gentle hand on Emily's shoulder. "You're a cop — or were — so you know perhaps more than anybody the answer to that question."

And she did. "You have to fight. For him, more than anybody else."

"For everyone," Steffy added. "What we do is for the good of everyone."

"I wouldn't be worth a salt if I didn't go out with my team and fight the threat of the Daemons. I take a risk, it's true. Every time I leave Armand there is the chance that he won't see me again. But I'd rather die in defense of my people — both Shikar and human — than sit at home doing nothing just to play it safe. Armand deserves better than that. The world deserves better than that."

"What if something should happen to you?" Emily pressed.

"The Shikars take care of their own. He would never want for anything, love or material or otherwise."

"We'll take care of you too, Emily," Steffy added. "You'll always have a place here now. No matter what happens. We're a family."

"A very big, very cool family," Cady said with a grin. "Just wait and see. Now. Would you go and fetch Edge, please? If I have to beat him I'm going to make him take a weapon out there with him tonight."

"Edge won't do it, Cady," Steffy warned her knowingly.

"He will. I don't care how good of a warrior he is, he needs to have some kind of weapon besides those blades of his. It's just the wise thing to do. Everyone else on our team carries at least a side arm now. Everyone but him, that is, the stubborn ass."

Emily didn't want to talk to Edge, not this soon after their confrontation last night. But she knew it would be childish of her to quibble against the order. And an order is what it was, even if Cady had said please. Emily was wise enough to know that just because Obsidian was the official leader of the group, it didn't mean that Cady wasn't a higher-ranking officer than she. Her orders were meant to be obeyed and without question. Emily wasn't about to start off on the wrong foot with the woman if she could help it. She liked Cady and Steffy already and didn't want to appear the coward in front of them.

"Do you know where I can find him?" she asked.

"He's still in his apartment, I think."

"And where is that, exactly?"

Cady's eyes twinkled devilishly. "Right next to yours."

Now that was a reply as unexpected as it was unwelcome to Emily, who merely gritted her teeth in aggravated response.

* * * * *

Emily took a deep breath as she stood before the large—and surprisingly beautiful—door to Edge's apartment. Her gaze roamed over the intricate carvings that adorned the thick, dark wood, seeing them without really registering what she saw. She was too nervy to appreciate the artwork before her. All of her thoughts were on Edge. On preparing herself to meet him face to face once again.

Her palms were damp. She raised one, fisted it, and knocked upon the door before she could change her mind.

"Enter," came Edge's curt but muffled response.

Emily took one more last, bracing breath, and opened the door. "Edge?" she called out, not seeing him anywhere in the foyer of his apartment. Her eyes were snared by a large bookshelf against one wall. It was as ornately carved as the door had been, only now Emily was fascinated enough by the craftsmanship to take in the details.

It was lovely, of that there was no doubt. The piece was comprised entirely of delicately rendered animals, hundreds of them, each in liquid stages of motion. Birds flew, monkeys climbed, and foxes ran. On and on the list of species went, until each figure blended in with the next, giving the bookshelf itself a sense of movement and animation. It was the most beautifully carved sculpture Emily had ever seen.

The most amazing thing, however, was not the bookshelf itself. It was what rested upon its many shelves. More carvings. Only these carvings were so amazingly realistic, so exquisitely beautiful, that they appeared to have been imbued with life itself. There were sculptures of wood, so many different kinds of wood that Emily couldn't even begin to guess the names of most of them. And there were sculptures of stone, soft and hard, smooth and rough, there were hundreds of different types. Not even in museums had Emily seen such fine craftsmanship.

A sculpture of three figures drew her eye. She approached it slowly, feeling as though she were in a dream, one comprised of such beauty that she feared herself unworthy of the visions it brought her. The carving was a rendering of a man, woman and child, with a cat nestled comfortably at their feet. The child was held between the couple, in swaddling clothes, with a shock of wild hair upon its head. The man was tall, so much taller than the woman that he appeared almost a giant in comparison. His shoulders were broad and strong, his stance one of arrogant pride. His hair was long and flowing down his back, though some of the strands tangled themselves with the hair of the woman in delicately rendered detail.

The woman commanded Emily's attention. She leaned closer to the sculpture, not daring to reach out and touch it, though her fingers fairly itched to do so. Why, the woman was Cady! Emily gasped. No doubt about it, this sculpture was one of Cady standing beside her husband, cradling her son between them. The depiction of the Shikar woman was so realistic that Emily almost expected the tiny eyes to blink, to see the swaddled baby squirm in its parents' embrace, or even hear the cat purring at their feet. It was amazing, like nothing Emily had ever seen.

"Emily?"

She realized with a start that Edge had been speaking to her for some time now, but she had been too ensnared by the sculpture to notice. Turning around with a guilty smile, she eased away from the bookshelf. The temptation to reach out and touch had become almost too much to bear. "Sorry?" she murmured.

"I asked why you were here," he prompted her.

Her eyes took him in and she felt an earthquake begin in the lower parts of her stomach. He was wet from his bath, with one large towel hanging over his shoulders and another draped negligently around his hips. His hair was longer, darker, when it was wet, hanging down to his buttocks. She gasped when he moved, the play of his muscles sensuously smooth and graceful. Her lips tingled. In that moment she wanted nothing more than to lick a path from his throat to his navel, sipping the drops of water that danced so temptingly upon his body as she did so.

She swallowed. Hard. "Cady wants to see you. At the armory." There was a moment for her to be grateful that those words had sounded much steadier than she felt...until he flung his hair about his broad shoulders. Impatient though his motion was — no doubt on his part an effort to fling excess water away — it slowed in Emily's eyes until she saw it dance around his luscious, damp body like a cape.

Emily almost fainted at the sight.

Edge seemed oblivious to her state. "I've told her countless times that I don't care for guns. They're far too slow and bulky," he growled.

That gorgeously toned body of his turned, granting Emily an unimpeded view of his firm backside beneath the towel. He bent over and gathered his boots, setting them before a cushioned chair. She felt her eyes boggle. He had the most amazingly sexy ass she'd ever seen and there was a moment for her to thank her lucky stars that the towel hid as much as it did, or else she would have jumped him then and there, begging him to take her.

"Well, she asked me to come and fetch you." Was she actually having this conversation? Was that her, sounding so nonchalant that even she wouldn't have realized her state of hypnotized obsession with his near-naked presence? That is, if she hadn't been inside her own body.

"As my lady wishes," he murmured, his voice so masculine, so potent and alluring that Emily actually took a step closer to him. Edge looked up at her, eyes shaded by his long dark lashes. "Would you mind helping me get ready? I still have to paint my armor on."

"Can't you get ready by yourself?" No way did she trust herself to get any closer to him than this.

"I can do most of my body without aid, but not my back and shoulders. Usually Obsidian helps but he's unfashionably late tonight." He snorted. "No doubt Cady has kept him away on purpose to punish me for some imagined slight. That woman loves to torture me."

Emily had a sinking feeling that he was wrong, that Cady had deliberately kept Sid away—not to punish Edge—but to force Emily into a close and intimate situation with him. "Fine, I'll help. But can we do this quickly? I don't want to be late for my first night on the job."

"We'll do this in the bathroom. I would hate to drip the stuff on the rugs."

Emily's toes curled in her boots, as if she could actually feel the thick piles of that carpet beneath her feet. Knowing she looked more docile than she felt, she followed him to the bathroom, watching the hypnotic sway of his wet hair over the muscled planes of his back as he led the way.

The bathroom here seemed no different in architecture to the one in her apartment. It was large, at least twice the size of the bathroom of her old apartment, with a sunken tub in the stone tiled floor, an oddly designed toilet that worked much the same as a human one, and a sink. But the decoration of the room was very much dissimilar from hers.

Instead of a functional faucet at the bath, the brushed metal was carved into a sweeping figure of a swan-necked dragon, lending it a decidedly oriental look. A matching faucet adorned the pot-bellied sink. The walls of the room were stone, as were the rest of the walls throughout the Shikar underworld, but they were adorned as ornately as the bookshelf in the foyer had been. Here, racing forms of the dragons, long wingless creatures with the gracefully long bodies of eels, swam through a splashing ocean of waves from the floor up to the ceiling. The images were carved into the very rock. The longer Emily stared at them, the more realistic they seemed.

They began to look as if they actually moved, stone though they may be.

And the ceiling, rising so high above that Emily couldn't fathom how the artist had carved there, was an exquisite work of art. Here, winged dragons held court over the wingless ones. Giant humanoid warriors rode upon their necks, raising spears and swords into the sky. Clouds served as perches for the great claws of the some dragons, while others dove and soared, their wings spread or even nearly folded in detailed stages of flight. Emily was overwhelmed with the sheer artistry of it all.

Edge prodded her with a pot of black, liquid armor. She came to herself with a start, seeking an excuse for her dumbfounded awe, but was saved the trouble. Edge seemed ignorant of her state, presenting her with a clear view of his back as he bent before her, sweeping his long hair aside. "Let's get this over with." His sigh was a curiously heavy sound.

"Look, if you'd rather I went and found Sid—"

"We cannot afford the delay. I'm sorry I sounded ungrateful. Please, I would be glad for the assistance." He rolled his broad shoulders, drawing her attention there insistently.

She hesitated, grasping the handle of the paintbrush with uncertain fingers. "Do I just slather it on as much I can?"

"Yes, the thicker the better. Leave no skin exposed."

"I still don't see how this is supposed to offer much protection," she mumbled half to herself.

"Agate has a way with clothing and materials. Her gifts are many, and it was only natural for her to search for an alternative to Cady's heavy bulletproof vests. Cady was the first of us to require armor, being as she was human when she joined us."

"What does being human have to do with needing physical protection?" Her eyes watched the hairs of the brush as they danced seductively over the smooth, taut muscles of his shoulders. She clenched her teeth against a moan and tried to focus on their conversation, though it was nearly impossible for her to do so.

Already she was that far under his spell, despite her better intentions.

"We Shikar are stronger. Our bodies can take much more damage than yours before we are laid low. We heal exponentially faster than you, and our healers have the ability to repair the most grievous of injuries when our bodies cannot heal themselves."

"Must be nice, not having to worry much about scrapes and bruises."

"Be that as it may, I still do not enjoy getting them." There was the hint of a smile in his voice. "You have an excellent right handed punch, by the way."

"You mean right hook." She couldn't help smiling.

"Right hook?"

"I'm not certain but I think its some kind of boxing term."

"Boxing?"

"Never mind. You know a lot about humans, I'll admit, but you don't know everything."

"I never said I did." His head turned to the side, giving her a tantalizing view of his sculpted profile behind the curtain of hair around it. "But I do like to pretend." He smiled.

Emily blinked. She would have laughed at his attempted humor, but he flexed his arms—his bicep and triceps muscles bulged mightily—and she was forced to catch her breath instead. He was wreaking havoc on her libido, something she'd not been completely prepared for considering her earlier anger with him.

Because of her discomfiture at her own raging hormones she refrained from further conversation for several minutes. The paintbrush stroked layers of black paint over his shoulders, back and waist as the silent moments stretched on. Too quickly for her to regain control of her senses, she was finished.

"Thank you." His voice was soft music in the silence as he turned and took the brush and pot from her.

"Who did all of these carvings?" She hadn't wanted to leave with her uncomfortable silence lying between them like a blanket. She asked the first thing that swept into her jumbled thoughts.

He looked about them long and thoughtfully before locking her gaze with his. "Do you like them?"

He hadn't answered her question.

"They're lovely," she admitted truthfully. Then it occurred to her, his silence telling more than he could have imagined. "You did them."

His lips curved in a tiny smile. "My Foils are not only useful on the battlefield."

"They can cut through stone then?"

"They are very strong, and unlike knives or other blades they do not need sharpening after much usage."

It surprised Emily to discover that such a vicious and deadly fighter as Edge surely was, he could still create these beautiful, ethereal sculptures. She would never have guessed him capable of such artistry. But then she knew little to nothing about him besides what she'd learned about him while on the battlefield.

She was coming to learn that he was a man of many facets.

Uncomfortable under his steady, burning gaze, she cleared her throat and turned to leave. "Well. I'll see you in the armory then."

It wasn't until she'd shut the door to Edge's apartments that she realized she had no idea where the armory was. She sighed in frustration and then laughed at herself. She'd have to make certain she avoided seeing Edge in a bath towel again any time soon or else he would end up thinking she was always this dim.

Heading off in the direction of Tryton's anteroom—the only direction she was as yet familiar with in this great place—she tried to ignore the images that flashed in her mind of Edge's wet and glistening body.

It was an effort in futility, though it grated on her nerves to admit it. Even if it was only to herself.

Chapter Nine

"The plan is to use whatever attraction Emily holds for the Daemons as a lure to capture at least one of them alive. Simple enough, eh?" Tryton stood at the head of a great stone table, while Obsidian's team of warriors—Emily now included in their number—sat with stunned looks on their faces.

All except The Traveler, whose features were hidden by the enormous dark cowl he always seemed to wear.

"Um…has that ever actually been tried before?" Cady asked with a dubious frown.

"We have captured some over the ages, but without much benefit to us. They were mindless husks, mere vessels for the rage and hungers that animated them. But now, I think, we should try again. Things have changed recently. The Daemons are evolving. Now is as good a time as any to try once more to learn from them what we may."

"If they can Travel now, how can we hope to keep one contained if we do manage to catch it?" Cady prodded.

"The very boundaries that serve to keep the Daemons out of our world will serve to keep them imprisoned here. Our only real concern is to keep them alive long enough to gather what information we can."

"Then it will be as you command, Elder." Obsidian rose and the rest followed as one, even Emily, who fel more than a little overwhelmed, surrounded as she was by these giant and fierce warriors.

Cady sidled up to Emily almost immediately. "You look a little nervous. Just follow our lead. We won't let anything happen to you."

Emily started. "I'm not worried about that at all. I can take care of myself—you forget, I've been doing this for the past week or so. While that doesn't necessarily make me as efficient as your group, I'm pretty sure I can keep myself alive." She sighed and rolled her shoulders, trying to loosen the tension gathering there. "I'm more nervous about appearing the professional in front of you all. This is my first night on the job. I want to leave a good impression."

Cady snorted. "I should've remembered. Despite your earlier protestations of arrogance, I can see now that you'll fit right in with the rest of us. And here I thought I was being maternal."

"You? Maternal towards me? Please tell me how you'd hoped for that." She laughed. "After all we're around the same age."

Cady merely stuck out her tongue—belying any claim to maternity she might have otherwise kept had she refrained from the childish impulse.

"Cady, Emily—come. We leave now." Obsidian's voice was a commanding whip.

Emily joined the group as they gathered around The Traveler. Everyone reached out and laid a hand on him, and Emily naturally followed their lead. There was a whooshing sensation in her ears. She grew lightheaded, slightly dizzy and, looking down, she saw the floor fall away from her feet and dim into nothingness.

Were they flying? She couldn't be sure. The Traveler's shoulder, where she'd placed her hand, was the only solid thing in this strange place. He didn't appear to be moving at all, while she felt completely cast adrift—as if she were hurtling through space.

Her sister would have loved this.

Now where had that thought come from? She hadn' thought about her younger sister in well over a year Emily had always found it was better not to dwell on unpleasant thoughts. But now, when her world was turning upside down—for better or for worse, she still could not attest—her only real thought was for her younger sister, who had so dearly loved being adventurous.

It seemed not even a split second had passed, though Emily's thoughts had been speedy and jumbled as if minutes had fled, when the world around her suddenly brightened. The group appeared on the edge of an apartment complex—an area Emily knew well for its apparently endless stream of domestic violence calls.

The smell of car exhaust and rotten garbage assailed her nostrils. This was not the best part of town to be in Still, the location would probably serve their purpose better than any other, she had to admit. No matter what kind of ruckus they caused, it was highly doubtful anyone would take real notice of it. The inhabitants of such places as this, Emily had learned long ago, were prone to look the other way whenever possible. No one here liked to borrow trouble.

"How in the hell are we going to accomplish this Sid?" Cady demanded.

Obsidian sighed deeply, a frustrated sound. "I haven't got a clue."

"Shit. It's hard enough to kill the damn things. I can't even begin to imagine how we're gonna actually catch one."

"Maybe we can just buy a really big dog crate and haul it home with us that way," Steffy offered with a shrug.

Cinder reached over and hauled Steffy up against his side, giving her a loud kiss on the temple. "Wow. Problem solved then. Well done, darling." He gave her a boyish wink with those facetious words.

Steffy rolled her eyes, but reached down and patted his buttocks lovingly.

Emily watched the entire exchange from a few feet away, though it felt as though she was a thousand miles removed from the scene. With instincts honed by years in police work, she studied their surroundings, being careful to note every possible entrance and exit should a Daemon choose to take them by surprise.

"Can we knock them out, maybe? Use tranquilizers or something?" Cady ventured.

"Their bodies are not biologically active, aside from their beating hearts. No drug will affect them." The Traveler answered her question, moving with the shadows to come and stand behind Emily as she walked the perimeter of the small copse of hedges in which they found themselves.

Emily tried not to feel stalked by the tall, dark man. Tried and failed.

"Well I'm fresh out of ideas, dammit. How have they been captured in the past, Traveler?"

"Bring them to me. Fight who you will to keep yourselves safe. I'll take care of the capturing."

"Well then. Emily, you ready to bring home the bacon?" Cady asked with a grin.

The woman enjoyed her work far too much it seemed.

"Sure." Emily's hand instinctively moved closer to the butt of her handgun.

"Just do what you've been doing, I guess. We're bound to run into some of the bastards before too long."

Emily stepped forward, intending to lead the group out of the copse. To where, she wasn't sure yet. She didn't think it mattered anyway. She'd just wander the streets until she came upon some threat. It may not be a glamorous plan, but it had worked for her this far. After only two steps, however, The Traveler's hand descended upon her like a weight, though his grip was gentle enough. Her vision dimmed and her heart thudded in her breast.

She tried to convince herself that she felt no fear at this man's touch.

He leaned in close, too closely for their audience to hear his soft words. "Tread carefully. If you should need help, call for me and I will come."

"Thanks, but I can handle this," she answered through gritted teeth. The Traveler's hand fell away, and it seemed her heart and lungs resumed their natural function. She sighed unsteadily and led the group deeper into the shadows of the buildings around them.

What a dangerous man this Traveler person was. Emily had noted that Cady seemed quite close to the strange being, but this obvious trust between the two was of no consolation to her, especially not after his visit last night. Could The Traveler be trusted? Was he really worried about her? And if so, why? What was his interest in her?

And how in the world could she get him to lose that interest, especially when she wasn't sure what had sparked it in the first place?

For the time being, she had no answers and a million other questions besides. But she'd be damned if she let it interfere with her purpose here right now. She was here to help discover this Daemon threat and the reasons behind it. That was all that should matter to her now. She vowed it would be all that mattered to her. Period.

* * * * *

Three a.m. rolled by and there was still no sign of the Daemons. The group of Shikars insisted that they take a short rest — Emily suspected they took the rest for her sake, as they looked as hale and hearty as ever while she felt completely burnt out. They sat perched on a street curb and Cady passed out small round pieces of fruit to each of them.

"Numese fruit. They're a variation of the apple family. The Shikars grow them in huge groves underground. I can't see how they live and bloom without natural sunlight but they seemed to do well enough without it," Cady supplied.

Emily took a tentative bite of the round, black fruit and was surprised by its deliciously sweet flavor. She finished hers first and Cady supplied her with a second.

"Shikars don't metabolize as fast as humans, therefore they don't eat as much or as often. Steffy and I still eat more than we probably should, hanging on to our human habits, I guess."

"Plus I like to eat just for the taste of food in general. I don't quite see it as fuel like Shikars do. Not yet anyway, and I rather hope I never do," Steffy said, her German accented words nearly unintelligible around a mouthful of fruit.

"Food is a necessity, like water or air," Obsidian said flatly.

"You big faker. I've seen you sneaking from my stash of chocolates, don't think I haven't," Cady threw out.

Obsidian smiled, looking sheepish. The expression changed his entire appearance and Emily was moved to notice how dashing and attractive he looked when he didn't look so stiffly righteous. "I didn't think you wouldn't notice. After all, you count every piece like they were precious gems."

Emily was jerked from her silent appraisal of the Shikar leader when Edge cleared his throat. She'd almost been able to ignore his presence in the past several hours. She'd certainly tried her best to, anyway.

Edge moved to sit next to her on the damp curb. His exceedingly long legs looked awkward in the position he chose, his knees up against his chest. Emily smiled slightly and he sighed, repositioning his legs so that they sprawled out before him.

"Being short has a few advantages," she admitted, gesturing to her own small stature.

"Yes, well, I daresay you could never win a foot race against me. Shorty." He smiled at last, his teeth flashing white in the dark.

Emily snorted. "What about the first night we met? I chased your ass down without any trouble." Her side had cramped for an hour afterwards, but he didn't need to know that.

"Ah. But I let you catch me then."

"What? No way. I caught you fair and square," she protested indignantly.

"I stopped running because I realized the Daemons would very likely attack you if I left you unprotected. I was right. They ran from me, but when you paused to shackle me, they came running back. To you. It was easier for me to take a stand while I kept you in my sight, protected."

"You ran for something like two miles. I caught you fair and square when you got tired of running and slowed down."

Cinder broke into their conversation then, laughing. "Edge is an excellent runner, Emily. He's fast and has a hell of a lot of endurance."

Emily rolled her eyes. "I should have expected one of you to stand up for his ego. I'm a pretty good runner too, you know. I was first in Track and Cross Country in my high school. Not to mention the police academy. It's not like Edge lost to just any old human girl."

"Yeah! You should see Em's body. It's a powerhouse. I'd kill for muscle tone like hers. I believe she could beat Edge's ass any old day she wanted," Steffy defended, flashing Emily a big, supportive smile.

Emily blushed as every male eye turned to her and looked her over from head to toe. Clearing her throat she tried to steer their attention away from her body. "Yes, well, he wasn't that easy to catch," she admitted.

"Edge can run a twenty-six mile marathon in under seven minutes. I don't think any human could outdistance that, no matter how good they are."

Steffy elbowed Cinder in the ribs and he winced. She sent Emily a sympathetic look in apology.

Emily looked sharply at Edge. "That's impossible," she scoffed.

"I'm a Shikar. Nothing is impossible."

Once again Emily snorted, but rose as she did this time so that she could look down upon him. She suddenly felt the need for some advantage, however imagined it was. "I'll believe it when I see it." She turned to the others as Edge rose at her side, making her heart race dizzyingly. He was standing so close she could smell him, a delicious mix of sandalwood and fresh, ozone-rich rainwater. She barely refrained from taking a long breath of his intoxicating scent. "I'm rested. Can we please get back to business?"

"Coward," Edge teased softly as she turned away from him.

Against her better judgment she turned and locked her gaze with his. "You wish."

His features softened and an expression akin to worry fleetingly crossed his face. "Yes, I do."

Emily started, taken aback as she was. "What?"

"I do wish you were a coward. Then you would not be here. You would be safe."

"I'm no more safe working the night beat as a cop than I am here with you guys," she gritted out disdainfully before turning and marching resolutely away from him.

So it was that she missed his last whispered words; not that he'd intended for her to hear them. "That's where you're wrong Emily, though I hope you never realize just how wrong."

The rest of the night, Emily avoided Edge like the plague. But every so often she would glance up and find his unflinching gaze resting on her. It took every ounce of willpower to ignore the shiver of awareness that raced down her spine whenever she caught him staring. But she managed. Just.

Chapter Ten

"We'll simply try again tomorrow night. And the night after that, and so on, until we succeed in our objective."

"Why don't we just take a trip to the Gates and see if we can't capture one there?"

Tryton appeared to give the idea some thought before shaking his head. "No, Cady. I want to use Emily as planned and you know she cannot survive those lands. I want one of the Daemons that have been after her, to see if they are any different from those that have come before."

"We shall try again tomorrow night, Elder," Obsidian promised.

The group parted, but Emily lagged behind with every intention of speaking to Tryton alone once more.

"Go and seek your rest, Emily." The Traveler came up at her elbow for he, too, had waited behind. "You'll get your chance for more questions later," he added, as if reading her mind.

Emily clenched her hands against the impulse to rip back that blasted cowl he wore. She hated talking to someone whose face she could not see. But she merely nodded her assent and turned to leave the room.

The long dark hallways of stone surrounded her like a womb as she meandered her way back towards her new apartment. It was so silent here one might never suspect that over a thousand Shikars called this place home. Emily had yet to see any faces other than those belonging to her teammates, but Cady and Steffy both had told her quite plainly that there were indeed many Shikars in this strange underground world. Men, women and children abounded...but the unattached Warriors lived on this side of the city, where Emily now lived. Like an odd military barracks.

The only sound was the weary tread of her own feet on the stone floor. Which is why it was so surprising when someone reached out from the shadows behind her and grabbed her arms in a strong, unbreakable grip.

Edge spun her around and backed her up against the nearest wall.

"You scared the shit out of me, Edge." She wriggled in his grip but his fingers only dug more deeply into her flesh, not hurting her — not yet — but holding her firmly in place.

He looked at her long and hard, causing her heart to trip with a sudden, elemental alarm, before swooping down to claim her lips in a kiss.

This was no gentle kiss. Nor was it merely a fiery, passionate one. This was a war on her senses, a war Edge had declared upon her, and the battleground was her mouth. He took her lips like a conqueror to the spoils. And with them he took her every sense and held them captive to his slightest erotic whim.

His lips were like fire on hers, sliding against hers with a power as ravaging as any flame set to timber. He gathered her so closely to him that she lost all breath but that which he gave to her from the depths of their kiss. He moaned against her mouth, a broken, desperate sound. Her heart fluttered.

Despite her surprise, despite all her promises to herself that she had no attraction to this man after the way he'd treated her, she felt herself melt into his bold embrace.

As her body softened, so did his fierce hold upon her. Where before he had sought to conquer, now he sought to coax, to tease, to seduce her into his possession. His tongue slipped passed her swollen and bruised lips to sample the secrets within, while gifting her with his own seductive flavor.

His thumbs brushed the sides of her breasts as his hands held fast to her upper arms. Her nipples immediately hardened into diamond bursts of sensation. His kiss deepened as if he sensed this response in her, and his erection pressed hot into the curve of her tummy. It was then she realized that he held her suspended off the floor with merely the strength of his hands and the tight press of his body against her. He was so strong.

But then so was she. Her stubborn will reasserted itself and she began to push against his embrace.

At last she tore free from his kiss, mouth swollen breath coming in short pants. "Let go of me," she gritted out, turning her face away when he would have moved in to resume their kiss.

He merely leaned down and licked a long hot line down the exposed curve of her neck. His mouth came to rest in the pulsing hollow of her throat, where he nuzzled her deliciously. Her knees would have given out if he hadn't been holding her off the floor.

"I said let go!" She bucked wildly against him and then had to bite back against a moan as her pubis rubbed erotically against the root of his hardness.

Edge pulled back with a feral sound of impatience. "I couldn't stand your ignoring me tonight."

"I ignored you because I didn't want anything to do with you. Especially anything like this."

"You lie. You're just as hot and wet for me now as you were the other night."

Emily shrieked indignantly and squirmed free of his hold. "I don't want anything to do with you, you jerk," she lied.

"Have me, Emily. Have all of me. I know you want me. Why fight so hard against our attraction? Why hold a grudge over my stupid words, when my actions are far more honest than my runaway tongue?"

"Because!" She cringed upon hearing her own childish response.

"I told you I was sorry for how I treated you. I did it because I was angry that I wanted you so much. There, that gives you power over me, knowing how much you affect me. Use that to your advantage, take me to your bed."

"I don't care how sorry you said you were. I never would have, uh, ooof, grrr!" she stuttered, all eloquence escaping her.

"Fucked me?" he supplied helpfully.

"Yeah! I never would have fucked you, if I had been thinking clearly. I was a mess. I hadn't slept for days. It was a huge mistake."

"Whether you intended to have me in such a swift, animalistic encounter is irrelevant. You wanted me. You still want me. Desire can cloud one's better judgment, but it rarely defies the goals of the heart. We would never have coupled if you hadn't felt some attraction to me. And there can be no doubt that I desire you." He gestured to the hard rise of his cock beneath the painted armor he wore, which did little to disguise his ardor. "Why fight against each other in this? It will gain us nothing."

"My heart is retarded. It doesn't know what it wants. My brain is the important part of me in all of this mess, and it's screaming at me to stay the hell away from you."

Edge grabbed her once more as she turned to flee. He pulled her by the wrist to face him, reaching up with his free hand to lightly stroke the side of her face. "I can't stop thinking about you." His voice cracked, and Emily felt her heart stutter in response. "About how you felt in my arms. I regret my angry words to you more than I can ever say. But I swear, I would do anything to make amends here and now."

"Make amends all you want. But that doesn't mean you'll ever get in my pants again."

"Did I make you so angry that you have lost all desire for me?" he demanded, jerking her tighter against him. He towered over her so that she felt dwarfed, but she faced him squarely, trying her best to ignore the wicked burn of his erection as it pressed against her.

And that quickly, her resolve crumbled. His eyes were Shikar eyes, but the emotions within them were naked and all too familiarly human. He wanted her, as much or more than he admitted. It was clear on his face, and in the tender anguish that swam in his gaze.

Emily felt her mouth tremble and fought to subdue the telltale evidence of her softening emotions. "We don't know each other, Edge. You have no idea what kind of person I am, nor I you. But one thing is for certain—you're not human, and I can't ignore that. Please…just forget about what happened between us. I'm not in the market for a lover and I know you don't want me—a human. For however brief a tryst we would share, our differences are too many to keep it light. Let it go."

"I haven't had my fill of you yet, and I won't let it go until I do," he said angrily.

Emily gritted her teeth and hissed out a long breath of air. "Now that's where you're always gonna lose with me, Edge. You let your temper get the better of you and then you take things just one step too far. The more I talk to you, the less I seem to like you." She pried his suddenly tight fingers away from her wrist. "And that does not bode well for your lame attempts at wooing me, now does it?"

"I'm sorry," he bit out, sounding not at all apologetic.

"Me too, Edge." She felt the need to strike out at him, to hurt him with words as he seemed so skilled. "Because you were the best piece of ass I've ever had. Too bad your personality isn't as attractive as your cock."

Turning away, she barely refrained from running back to her room.

She missed the diamond hard look that entered his eyes. Missed the telltale signs of an aggressive male picking up the gauntlet she had just thrown between them with those parting words. It was probably better that she had missed them, else she really would have broken into a run despite all her efforts not to.

Chapter Eleven

It was early—still daylight in New York City—when Emily rose from her bed. She hadn't slept much, only a few hours, but it was better sleep than she had been getting and she was grateful for it. Most of the other Shikars on her team would probably still be asleep, synchronizing their hours to those of the region they were assigned to protect.

Therefore it came as some small surprise to Emily when she heard a soft knocking upon her door.

As soon as Emily moved to open it, the door flew open itself to reveal a tall redhead with wide flaming eyes.

"Oh my! So you're Emily. It is so great to finally meet you, to see you in person. Wow, your eyes are so blue! Are those your real eyes or contacts? I have always wanted a pair of contacts, but The Elder won't let me buy them. Not that I would wear them; we Shikars don't have weak vision—not that I am saying you do but... Oh, I am just so excited to meet you!"

The woman spoke a million miles an hour and barely seemed to pause for a breath. Her tall stature and extra-full curves made Emily, for once, feel like a dowd. Emily immediately liked her, even if she was a bit overcome by the woman's enthusiasm.

Without preamble the woman stepped in, moving immediately to a stack of romance novels on the coffee table. "Wow! The new Lora Leigh—can I read this when you are finished? I have to get rid of my books once I am through—else someone might know I have been on the surface—but now that you are here I can just say I borrowed them all from you and keep them forever. Cady and Steffy don't read that much anymore because their husbands get all cranky when they take any time away from them. Males are such babies. Now that you are with Edge, I guess you will stop reading too."

Emily reeled. "I'm sorry. What did you say your name was?"

The woman blushed and grew flustered. "Oh I am so sorry. I am called Agate. I make your armor and your clothes—well, some of them. Steffy helps. She does get so bored around here when Cinder goes out without her— which is not that much anymore now that she is finished with most of her training. What I would not give to train to be a warrior—but I do not have any real Caste traits strong enough for use in battle, beyond Traveling. Though I suppose I must have some talents I have yet to discover. I mean, after all, my eyes are still Shikar red and not Traveler black. Only multiple Castes keep their birth eye color. Wouldn't it be great if I woke up one morning with a full-blown Caste like a Foil master or Incinerator? But then I have never heard of such a gift in a Shikar woman. As far as I know there are few Caste traits to be had among us, and most of the women won't even admit to possessing them."

"It's good to meet you, Agate." Emily couldn't think of anything else to say. Not that it mattered; Agate spoke enough to fill up any real silence.

"I know I am talking a lot, but I have just been so excited about meeting you. After you emailed us and told us you were fighting the Daemons—another human warrior-woman! —I knew you would come to us, and so you have."

Emily laughed and plunked down on her overstuffed sofa beside the quicksilver woman. "What are you talking about? What email?" Emily asked, bewildered and amused.

"Your email to the Voyeurs, silly! We women are the Voyeurs. Though, I guess I shouldn't tell you until The Elder gives me permission. But I know he will so I will pretend he already has."

"Wait a minute. You run the Voyeurs website?" Curiouser and curiouser.

"Oh yeah! It was Steffy's idea, of course. She is the web savvy one and she built the site. We use it as a tool to keep tabs on what is going on with Daemon sightings here and there in the human world. It has come in quite handy since we put it up. We keep our purpose in it a secret, and pretend we are just researchers interested in the Daemons, but when humans like you email us we usually investigate the goings on. It is our job, you know."

"No, I didn't," Emily said weakly. The Shikars were a surprising and complicated bunch; that much was certain.

"Oh well, not everyone knows. Only the Council, and a select few of The Elder's closest warriors. Some of our women are even married—I did say that only Shikar women, and select ones at that, were Voyeurs, didn't I? —and not even their husbands know. Can you believe that! It's like we are in the F.B.A. or the C.I.I. with all of this top secret agent stuff."

Emily laughed. "You mean the F.B.I. and C.I.A."

"Yeah, that is what I said. F.B.I. and C.I.A. Oh! I meant to ask. Do you have any shoes? I love looking at human shoes. I have designed some footwear myself based on your Prada designer. But the only real use they have, or so Cady tells me, is in the bedroom. I am thinking about designing some sex-only shoes, you know, for the mated couples' fun. I am not mated, thank goodness, but it is a great time consumer to design sex toys and negligees and what have you, when I am bored. I designed the Mone. You should ask Edge about it the next time you are having fun together. He's got one—"

Emily managed, at last, to interrupt. "Does everyone know about me and Edge? Good grief, can't a girl have one fling without the entire world knowing?"

Agate laughed. "Not everyone knows, silly. Just a few of us girls. We share most everything. Desondra is the one who originally found out. She has visions, you know. She admitted to me that after seeing you guys in that particular vision, she had to seek out her husband and it was hours before they left their bedroom." Agate laughed and giggled like a young girl.

And Emily supposed she probably was young. With the Shikars, it was almost impossible to tell their age by their appearance, as Emily had quickly learned over the past couple of days.

"Well, I know you will want to get ready for tonight, so I'll leave. Can I come back later? I will know when not to disturb you, I can sense when you are sleeping—you do not sleep nearly as much as you should—but when you are awake can I come for a visit?"

"Sure. But how can you know when I'm asleep—"

Agate laughed and bounced up from her seat. "Oh I know lots of things. It is just the way I am made." She giggled. "Please don't look so wary, I would never pry where I do not belong. That is Desondra's job." She laughed again and bounced towards the door. "It was so good to meet you, Emily. Will you become a Shikar like Cady and Steffy, do you think? Edge needs a strong woman like you. He is such a handful. Oh, I am very, very glad you're here!"

Emily smiled and grabbed the discarded Lora Leigh paperback, holding it out to Agate. "Here, you can read it. I've already read it twice myself."

Agate's eyes widened and she grabbed the book as if afraid that Emily might renege on her offer. "Thank you, thank you! I absolutely cannot wait to read it."

"Have fun." Emily waved her off, but the mercurial Agate was already through the door.

What a fountain of information that Agate was. And what an odd way to start the day, Emily thought with a grin. Now she was as curious to learn about her new family as ever. Perhaps even more so.

* * * * *

Tryton answered his door before she even had time to knock. "I thought you might come today, Emily. Come inside." He motioned her forward and stepped aside to allow her to enter.

"I'm not going to ask how you knew I'd be here," she said with a smile.

"Your curiosity is written all over you whenever you don't think anyone is looking. And since I am the head of this ragtag family, it stands to reason you would see me as the fount of any information you might require. Have a seat, please." He himself went to one of the overstuffed leather chairs and sank down with a sigh.

Emily sat as well. "Agate visited me. It seems you've got quite a sting operation going on between my world and this. I never in a million years would have thought the Shikars had a web presence." She grinned.

"This is your world now, Emily. You'll get used to it soon, I hope. And as for the Voyeurs—mum is the word, or so Cady would say. Only a few know of their existence, or purpose."

"I know. Agate told me. Don't worry, I'm pretty good at keeping quiet."

"I've no doubt." He eyed her comically. "So. I know you've questions. I'll answer as I may, but any one of my people would be quick to tell you that I am the most cryptic of the bunch."

"I've seen that for myself already. Actually, I just came to ask you about The Traveler." Emily looked about nervously. "He's not around is he?"

"No. We are alone, and none may see that which I do not wish to reveal. So don't worry about anyone spying," he said blithely.

Emily grinned wryly. "Well, I've come to learn that you can never be too sure of privacy around here."

Tryton laughed. "So what do you wish to know?"

"Who is he? He's so weird. So different from everybody else."

"He is different. But then, he is very old and with age one tends to get a little..." He seemed to search for the right word.

"Eccentric," she supplied.

"Exactly," he responded with a smile. "He is very powerful. But also very secretive. You need have no fear. He is entirely trustworthy."

"How did you know I was wondering about that?"

"I thought you knew better than to ask," he teased. "But in this instance, I don't need any hidden gifts to know. Everyone wonders about The Traveler when they first meet him. He has his secrets—we all do—but they are not withheld maliciously or with any dark purpose. He merely keeps to himself."

"He came to me, my first night here. It made me a little...nervous," she finally ended.

Tryton frowned. "Did he tell you why he visited you?"

"He said he was worried about me."

"Ah. He has ever had a soft spot for humans—even more than I—not that he'd admit it. And you would seem all the more fragile to him because of your lack of psychic power, whereas Cady and Steffy came to us with their own gifts."

"He said I reminded him of someone. A woman. What did he mean by that? Did he have a wife or something?"

Tryton was silent for a long while. "No, he has never mated. And for once, truthfully, I'm not sure I know the answer to your question. The Traveler can keep his secrets buried deep, even from me it would seem. Perhaps it would be best for you to ask him this question."

"He would never answer me."

"Are you sure?" Tryton pressed.

"Look, if you don't want to tell me, that's fine. It's no big deal, I was just curious."

Tryton nodded. "I have noticed that humans are very curious people. But I think you're wrong about him. I think, if you asked, The Traveler would tell you much that you might wish to know about him. It appears he has been far more open with you, in speaking of this mystery woman, than he has been with anyone else."

Emily highly doubted it, but let the subject drop. "I've another matter to discuss with you."

"I have no doubt you have many more than one," he allowed with a small twitch at the corners of his mouth.

"One will do for now," she chuckled. "About this change from human to Shikar—"

Tryton sobered immediately. "Do not even think on it further. You are not psychic and it cannot be done for you."

"How do you know?" she pressed.

"I just know."

"Has anyone ever tried it?"

Tryton's hands clenched into fists. "Of course it has been tried! Our people have not always been so reclusive. But such a thing is against the nature of our two species. It is only through chance, merest chance, that any have survived such an ordeal as the changeover from human to Shikar."

"I just can't believe it all has to do with the psychic mumbo jumbo everyone swears on."

Tryton's eyes were hard as nails, and hot as flame as he stared her down with his gaze. "Well, believe it and think no more on it. I have seen too much heartbreak over failed conversions, witnessed too many mistakes made over the eons between our two races. Attempting to change without some psychic gifts is folly. Damn your eyes, it is folly to attempt such a thing even with such gifts!"

"I never said I would attempt it. But the possibilities are amazing. To have the power of your people... It would—"

"The Shikars do have power. But it is not for the likes of you."

Emily bristled, trying and failing not to take offense. "What if you're wrong? What if it isn't just psychic ability that sustains the human soul during the change? What if you're too blind to see what's so clearly before your face that you've overlooked—"

"Do you not think I know all there is to know about my race? I have lived for centuries, for hundreds of human life spans. Believe me, I know. Allow me to share something with you, little human." He leaned forward intently, orange-yellow eyes stormy. "A long time ago, when our people were still living in the sun of your world, when your race was young and lived in our protection, there was a man who tried to do what you are suggesting.

"It was folly. But he was in love. And our kind does not love so lightly as yours. When we love it is so deep a love as to blind us to all other truths. He loved a maiden, a human maiden with all the frailty and selfish cruelties your kind can possess. Wanting to be with her, he lay with her in passion and in love. He loved her and filled her with his seed.

"No Shikar man had ever mated with a human, not until then. And it surprised us all when she was poisoned by the essence of her lover. She faded, and despite all his efforts — for this man was a great and powerful warrior — the woman died in the arms of her lover.

"In a rage of pain and despair, the man unleashed his power onto the Earth with a vengeance, destroying much that could never be regained in his sorrow. One warrior, out of love for the wounded man, came forth and tried to stop the destruction wrought from his brethren's broken heart. But Shikar turned on Shikar, and a great battle was waged.

"All of humanity fled from Shikar in terror in the aftermath of such violence. Our kind retreated from the world entirely, and from that day to this, any unprotected sex between our races has been forbidden, to prevent such tragedy from ever happening again. Over time, there have been those who sought to test fate and the law was broken...but until Cady no human woman survived such an encounter."

Emily was shaken at the pain the memory seemed to cause him and was ashamed that she had helped to dredge up such a dismal recollection. "What about human men?" She couldn't help asking. Did human men fall dead in the arms of a female Shikar's embrace, she wondered.

"Human men are safe from Shikar females. It is the semen of a Shikar male that is deadly."

"How odd. And you have no ideas why?" she pressed.

"It is Nature's whim, an evolutionary trait. And it is simply the way of things. Not everything can be neatly defined or explained. Seeing what you've seen, knowing all that you do now, can you have any doubt of that? Some things just are. We Shikar are warriors. We do what we must to protect our races from destruction. What more do we need to know than that?"

"Everything. It is by understanding ourselves and those around us that we can hope to win anything worth saving."

Tryton eyed her darkly but said nothing, clearly tied up in his own ideology.

"You know what I think," she continued. "I think you've lived for so long you've become blind to new ideas. You don't want to believe that things change and that surprises are not impossible in this world, even for your species. Especially for your species."

"And I think you talk too much," he said, but with a fond smile that took the sting out of his words. "You and Cady and Steffy all talk too much. It must be a human trait."

"No. You're just lucky with us three, that's all," she teased, but in her mind she wondered. Oh how she wondered at all the possibilities...

Chapter Twelve

Emily wasn't at all surprised when it fell on her to apply Edge's armor once again that evening. She'd known Cady was a devil, but she'd truly underestimated the woman's perseverance as a matchmaker. This time, after Cady had painted the armor over Emily's nude and freshly shaven body, she had simply handed the can of black gunk over with a smile.

"Edge will be waiting," she said with a wink. "Take your time, of course. It's early yet."

Emily had growled, but she'd complied. Far be it from her to allow room for anyone to malign her courage...even if she was nervous as hell by the time she reached Edge's chambers. No one needed to know but her how badly her hands shook as she twisted the handle of the door and entered.

But she almost dropped the can of armor paint when she saw Edge standing, completely nude, and waiting for her.

God, he was just as big as she remembered! "Jeez, put a towel on, will you?" she managed in a deceptively bored—if a little bit shaky—voice. It was difficult but she finally found the strength of will to tear her eyes away from his glorious cock.

Which was, of course, completely erect.

"I've been waiting for you, Emily."

"I can see that." She fidgeted, then stilled as she saw him smile at her telltale movement. "Come on, quit playing. Let's just get this over with." She lifted the can and paint brush.

Edge strode forward and took them from her weak hands. He sat them on a nearby table—yet another stunning creation of lifelike carvings—and turned back, placing his hands gently on her shoulders. His skin burned hers through its shiny black covering.

"I want you," he said huskily.

"Please don't, Edge," she pleaded. "I can't."

He pulled her close. "Why not?" he asked, lowering his mouth to her upturned face.

"It won't work out between us."

"We will never know for sure, unless we try it and find out," he murmured before his lips met hers in a soft caress.

He parted her lips and slipped his tongue gently inside. Emily sighed, feeling all her resistance fade away into nothing. She sucked his tongue as it danced along hers and let her arms twine about his neck as they were wont to do.

"You taste so good," he whispered. "You feel incredible in my arms."

"So do you," she answered, running her fingers through his hair, which was still damp from his bath and smelling strongly of sandalwood. "God, I love your hair," she moaned.

He licked her lips sensually and pulled her up against the fierce demand of his erection. "We Shikar are not as well furred as your human men. But we take pride in our hair, our glorious crown." He smiled against her mouth.

Emily giggled and blushed at the sound. "What about Cinder, then? His hair is really short. Doesn't he want a glorious crown?" she teased.

"Ha! The young pup has shorn locks because they were singed off in a training session with one of the student Incinerators. He keeps them short now to prevent another accident—though if you asked him, he'd merely say its more stylish a look for him this way." He nuzzled her neck playfully. "Enough about him; talk only about me now."

Emily laughed and Edge squeezed her tightly against him. His bare chest glistened and she kissed it, much to Edge's pleasure—if his hungry growl of a response was any indication. Wanting to explore, she ran her hands over the smooth muscled planes of his body and bent her head to one small, hard male nipple.

The tiny, pebbled nipple was hairless, as was the rest of him, and Emily licked it teasingly. Edge inhaled sharply and his hands dug into her rear, raising her up higher against his cock. Ever so gently, she bit down on the sensitive flesh and was pleased to feel him tremble against her with the force of his growing need.

Surprising her, Edge lifted her and carried her to a divan at the far end of the room. He tossed her gently onto its cushions and followed her down, lying heavily upon her. "I need you," he said, rocking his hips into the cradle of hers.

"But I've got my armor on already," she complained, but only half-heartedly. "It would take too long to put it back on, wouldn't it?"

"Damn it," he growled, "you're right. Well, there are countless ways to love." He smiled wickedly down at her. "Let me show you one."

Divesting her of the clothes she wore over the risqué armor paint, Edge soon had her shining black body bared to his gaze. "You know, this has possibilities," he mused aloud. "Woman, I love the way you look in this."

And Emily had known he would. While Steffy seemed nonchalant about wearing her armor and nothing else, both Cady and Emily were more reserved. The rubbery covering looked exactly like liquid latex once dried, and offered no room for modesty.

Beneath their covering of shining, rubbery black, Emily's nipples peaked demandingly before Edge's gaze. When he leaned down and licked them, Emily was shocked to feel the warmth of his tongue sear her flesh as if it were completely nude. Reflexively, she arched up for more of the sweet torture.

Chuckling at her response, Edge dipped his head in for a second taste, and pulled her breast deep into his mouth. Sucking and biting on one nipple, his fingers pulled and pinched the other until she was gasping with every sweet move he made on her.

Wrapping her legs around his waist, she arched up fully against him. The hard flesh of his sex ground against her pelvis. She grew wetter and wetter, undulating against him until they were both trembling and straining for more. Rubbing her hands against the broad muscles of his back, she pulled his head closer against her breast and he rooted even more deeply.

His hair was a cool spill of silk over her face and chest as he moved. Still rocking her hips into his, still clutching him tightly against her very heart, she rained kisses down upon his head and temples.

"I was a fool, Emily. A complete fool," he said raggedly, rubbing his face against the full mound of her breast. He rocked his cock tight into the cradle of her pussy, which was wet and needy beneath the barrier of her armor.

"Me too," she admitted, wrapping her legs more tightly around him, meeting his thrusts with her own.

"I am a warrior, Emily, first and foremost. I do not want to lose myself in you. I cannot." His voice broke.

Emily lifted his face to hers. "You'll always be a warrior. And so will I. This attraction between us won't change that."

"I need you so much. You make me feel too much. Far too much to keep this light," he admitted, kissing her over and over as if helpless not to.

His words frightened and thrilled her. To move so fast into such unexplored territory gave her pause...but only just. "I need you too, Edge. Beyond that, nothing else matters right now. We'll take it one step at a time, okay?"

His gaze met hers, dark and worried. The movement of his hips stilled. "You cannot be a Shikar. Not if what Tryton believes is true. What I feel for you will not pass in only one short human lifetime, and that is all we can share between us as things stand. I know it. You should know it too."

"We'll cross that bridge when we come to it," Emily said shakily.

"I knew that first night between us would only make me want a thousand more like it."

Tears filled her eyes. "Me too."

He kissed her, long and deep, and resumed his movements upon her. Rocking gently between her legs, he gathered her more closely to him than ever before. "Come with me, Emily. Come with me now," he commanded.

The angle of his thrusts against her rubbed her swollen clitoris with exquisite pressure. Even without penetration or even skin-to-skin contact between them, Emily felt herself flying into the face of an orgasm with alarming ease.

"Oh, baby, I'm coming," he breathed against her mouth. "I'm coming."

The hot splash of his semen against her sex was the catalyst she needed. With a cry that Edge swallowed with his kiss, she came undone in his arms. The climax was long and wicked. Like a storm over the sea, it washed over her, drowning her, until at last she was spent, limp and damp beneath him.

"Next time, we'll be naked, you and I. Though I'm not sure I could stand the intensity," he said with a grin.

"Promises, promises," she laughed.

Edge moved off of her and gently helped her to her feet. Her knees were weak, her body singing in the aftermath of her pleasure. Bending her back over his arm, Edge kissed her long and deep. His mouth ate at hers, his tongue sliding along hers with slow, delicious heat.

"Come on. Let's get cleaned up. I'm eager for our duties of the night to end and for our true pleasures to begin," he murmured, his dark sensuality washing over her in intoxicating waves.

It was a perfect interlude, one she hadn't expected with this man, but one she would treasure all the more because of it. Edge was a man of unfathomed depths, and the more she learned about him, the more she wondered. He had the ability to make her mad as hell, or content as a well-fed kitten. There'd never been anyone in her life that could make her feel as much as this man was able to. It was surprising. It was exciting. And it was wonderful.

But as she cleaned the warm bath of Edge's come from her belly and thighs, as she bantered back and forth with him, smiling and laughing more than she had in ages, she began to think on the possibilities. She began to wonder.

Dangerous though it was, she began to plan.

Chapter Thirteen

Something was amiss in the dark shadows of the night. For three hours Emily had taken the Shikar team with her deep into the bowels of her beloved city, and though there had been no sign of Daemons, there was an ominous feeling in the air as they searched.

Cady stilled and the entire party halted, waiting. Her face was a study of concentration and after several minutes—long minutes that felt more like hours to Emily who was unaccustomed to the ways of a Shikar Hunter—she finally broke the silence. "We're being watched. And followed."

Obsidian looked around, studying the darkness that surrounded them. "I feel them too. I have for the past hour. But why do they not attack? We are giving them ample opportunity."

"I don't know," Cady answered thoughtfully.

"Maybe they know we're up to something," Emily offered.

Edge had been at her side all evening. He put his hand on her shoulder possessively and pulled her tight against his side. "I doubt it. Daemons are none too bright."

"Maybe they're getting smarter." She tried not to settle against him, but gave up after only a few seconds. It was too delicious, having him so close.

The Traveler, who had also stayed with the group—an unusual occurrence from what Emily understood, as he usually preferred to blip in and out whenever the whim took him — seemed to ponder this. "Perhaps."

Cady laughed derisively. "No way. What would they do, go to monster school and get some book smarts? I doubt it. They're just waiting for something."

"Maybe they wait for orders from their commanders, such as they are," Cinder offered.

"Let's keep walking. Maybe they'll attack soon. We just need to keep our cool and wait them out." Cady motioned for Emily to lead on.

No sooner had she finished her statement than a group of Daemons swarmed into the night. The battle, it seemed, was on.

Faster than her human eyes could follow, Emily watched The Traveler come forth and immediately choose his prisoner. Through the fray he walked, as if the surrounding violence affected him not at all. Still and calm beneath his billowing cloak, he reached out to one of the hulking beasts and laid his powerful hand upon it. The monster lashed out with a howl of rage. A quick blink and they both disappeared, leaving Emily to gasp, wondering how The Traveler would fare against such an attack wherever he was.

At her back, fighting off one of the Daemons, Edge called out to her. "Don't worry about him. He's better off than we are."

More and more of the Daemons crowded into the night, Traveling from their world with horrifying ease. Outnumbered as they were, Emily rethought their position in the crowded city alleys. She fought her way to Obsidian, firing her handguns into the gaping maws of her enemy whenever they strayed too close, batting them out of the way with the butt of the weapons when she ran out of ammunition.

"We need to get to open ground. They'll only swamp us if we stay here." She turned as a monster attacked her from the side, but needn't have bothered. One of Edge's foils glinted through the night and beheaded the foul creature before it had the chance to lay one claw on her.

They grinned at each other over the din.

"We cannot afford to be seen by your people," Obsidian shouted, hacking away at his enemies even as he answered.

"We won't," she promised, reloading her weapons as quickly as she was able. "There's a playground nearby. I can get us there without anyone seeing. I know a shortcut that avoids the streets."

"But won't we be seen from this playing ground?" he asked, sounding somewhat harried but otherwise unconcerned that he was surrounded by blood, carnage and not a little bit of violence.

"There are trees. Leafy trees all around the perimeter, and if anyone looks out their apartment window that's all they should see."

"Lead on then," he commanded. "Everyone, to Emily. Follow her!"

She led them away from the fray, but not after being slowed by three Daemons seeking to waylay her. Though bullets could only really slow them down, she fired over and over until they fell away, leaving them to be dispatched by the Incinerators. Behind her, Cinder burned the fallen corpses and set fire to those still standing that he could reach.

And Cady, well, she was as volatile in the midst of battle as she was in every other aspect of her life. Appearing as if she was throwing napalm from her hands, she felled Daemon after Daemon with a smile on her face. Her laughter rang out in the night, a stark contrast to the monsters' shrieks and grunts of battle. Emily had never seen anything quite like it. No wonder everyone loved the warrior woman. Nothing ever seemed to faze her.

Turning away from the alley, she took the group of Shikars in a direction she hoped would offer them better leverage against their enemies. Though she hadn't bothered to count, she'd known the odds were greatly stacked against them. The Daemons' numbers seemed inexhaustible…and there were only six of them to stand against what was turning out to be an army.

"Almost there," she called to those who followed. Edge stayed right beside her and his presence was a great comfort to her. As if sensing her thoughts had turned to him, he reach out and took her hand as they ran.

There was a break in the maze of buildings at last. Beyond it, an unkempt playground lay in wait beyond a copse of tall oak trees. It offered some small bit of safety to the battle-primed group of warriors. It would be far easier to fight their enemies on open ground.

Steffy, blades glowing from her hands, engaged a group of three monsters that followed them from the alley. Slicing them to tiny pieces, as if she'd been doing such things all her life, her assistance made it easier for Obsidian, Edge, and Emily to cross to the playground unhindered.

"Should we leave to get reinforcements?" Emily asked, knowing that Obsidian had the power to Travel them out of danger.

"No. There are no backup teams that are trained fight in the Territories as we do. Those that have such training are out in other lands tonight."

"The Shikars are spread pretty thin," she murmured.

Close as he was at her side, Edge heard her quiet words. "You have no idea."

It was quiet for long moments, the Daemons presumably still far behind them. "Will they follow?" Steffy asked.

"They will follow. For whatever reason, they want Emily," Obsidian growled. "They want her very badly." His gaze burned into hers, studying her thoughtfully as if she were a puzzle to solve.

But the time for rest passed as quickly as it had come. Their reprieve had not lasted long. Cinder streaked out from the alley, billowing flame behind him. Facing the Daemons that followed him the group failed to notice the adversaries that Traveled into being directly behind them.

"Shit!" Emily screamed as a clawed hand fell heavily, slimily upon her. Her vision dimmed as the monster prepared to Travel.

And then the dizziness passed. The Daemon's arm dangled from her T-shirt, then fell to the ground. Edge stepped between her and the Daemon—whose arm he'd just neatly severed—and sliced it to ribbons with long talons that shot in a blue-white glow from his fingertips.

The group of Shikars flew into action, beating away at the Daemons who swarmed in from every front. The ground was wet with the black tar of their blood, the playground littered with their bodies—which Cinder was quick in burning. And still more came at them.

Edge was surrounded by the beasts. Emily retrieved a large bowie knife from a sheath in her belt and ran forth to help him. She was grateful for the protection of her armor, for even though the Daemons weakened before her—still unwilling to harm her—she was battered and bruised all the same as she met them head on.

It was hard, but she knew she must not let them touch her for longer than an instant or they would take her. Their way of Travel was different from a Shikar's in that it took longer and was not as precise, or so it seemed as they appeared willy-nilly all over the battlefield, but given more than a second or two they would have had her. It was terrifying, but it fueled the fighting instinct within her so that she held her own in the midst of the seasoned warriors that made up her team.

And then, as quickly as they came, the flood of Daemons abated. Only a few remained and with a burst of glittering, boomeranging blades from Edge's hands, the threat these stragglers posed was over and done with in seconds. Cinder burned the bodies and the team regrouped amidst the chaos of the flames.

As the night fell silent once more, the team prepared to leave. But Obsidian's words stopped them cold.

"Where is Cady?"

Emily looked around, but the warrior woman was nowhere to be found. The burning bodies that littered the playground, already turning to ash in the sand, all belonged to the Daemons. Cady was missing.

"*Where the hell is my mate?*" Obsidian's shout was a howl in the night air. But Cady did not come.

* * * * *

Cady followed close behind her team as Emily led them through the maze of alleys. Careful to keep them within sight, she made sure that every possible scrap of evidence was burned to ash on the ground. Reveling as she always did in her Shikar strength and power, she threw out flame after flame to eat away at the Daemons who came to engage her.

Compared to the fifteen years she'd spent killing these beasts as a human, being an Incinerator was a piece of cake. Nothing was easier—or more amusing, she had to admit—than flame bombing her enemies in the thick of battle. Though Cinder was far more skilled than she, it was a game between them to keep tally of their kills and compare them after the night's battling was done.

So far she'd taken out thirty-one beasts on her own. Thirty-one! Who'd have thought a quiet, small-town bookseller like herself would ever be capable of such carnage? And with a smile on her face, no less.

She laughed darkly and tossed a ball of fire onto the Daemon corpse lying at her feet. Surveying her work with a keen eye, she didn't notice when two monsters came up behind her.

With a mighty and brutal kick one of the Daemons sent her legs flying out from beneath her. The other fell on her and bit the arm she used to flail out at it. She screamed as its wicked fangs sank deep into the muscle of her forearm. She kicked out and sent the first Daemon flying, but no matter how hard she tried she could not shake free of the one who held her clamped between its jaws.

"Let go, goddamn it!" she screamed, beating it about the head with her free arm and trying desperately to regain her feet.

The fire that slept inside of her, dormant but ever watchful, leapt forth and sent a shield of flame around her arm. But the Daemon held, instinctively knowing that in doing so it was safer than in letting her go. It dug its teeth into her flesh, crunching her bone with its powerful jaws even as its claws sank into her shoulder and hand to better keep its grip on her.

"Motherfucker!" The pain wrenched a scream from her and she struggled to throw the beast off, uncaring that her arm was further mangled through her own protests. The Foils in her captured arm would only have anchored the beast tighter to her, so she sent her other hand — now tipped with glowing white-blue blades — deep into the belly of the beast. She wanted the bastard off of her and she wanted it off now.

And then it was gone. But not through her own machinations.

With a loud sighing *'poof'* the Daemon turned to dust before her eyes. Not hide nor hair of it was left behind, only fine black silt that smelt of long decayed death.

A black-cloaked man, features obscured by a deep and billowing cowl, bent down over her. "Grimm. Thank God —"

But it wasn't Grimm.

Cady's eyes widened and her heart nearly burst from her chest. "Who are you?" She began to crawl backward, away from the stranger in a motion of self-defense, but the man followed and bent down at her side.

His hand gently touched the side of her face and was both cold and warm at the same time. Cady shivered and searched for some clue as to who he was, but his face remained firmly in the shadow. "Cady," the man's smooth voice murmured softly, causing chills to run up and down her spine. His hand then moved down to her injured arm.

In an instinctive reaction, Cady flinched, though she needn't have done so. The man's touch was gentle, and the moment he laid his hand upon her wound, the pain lessened considerably. She breathed a sigh at the sudden, unexpected relief.

"Cady!" Obsidian's voice had the dark man's head shooting up, and he stepped away from her alertly. "Cady!"

The man gave her a long last look, then disappeared, leaving her gasping in his wake.

Obsidian fell down on his knees beside her. "Oh baby, you're hurt. Just lie still, I'll take care of you. We must get this healed. Are you okay? Say something." He gripped her hard against his heart, which thundered deafeningly against her ear.

Cady felt the shock of blood loss and pain set in heavily upon her. As if in a dream she pointed with her good arm to where the dark man had stood but mere seconds before. "Did you see him? Did you see? Who was that?"

"Who, darling? There's no one there." Obsidian tried his best to soothe her as she began to grow limp in his arms. "Take hold of me, everyone. We're leaving *now*."

Cady felt the din of Travel surround her as Sid took her home to safety. "Who was that? Who...he saved me," she breathed before oblivion took her.

Chapter Fourteen

As Cady was being healed by her husband after being hypnotized into a deep slumber by the mere sound of his voice, Emily and Edge made their way to the chamber where Tryton and The Traveler were interrogating their prisoner.

It had been a long and harrowing night for their team, and they were lucky that only one of them had sustained any real injuries. Emily felt the strain of being the only human of the group. While she had managed to keep up with the fighting, she hadn't the stamina or the strength to take on as many Daemons as the others could so easily. Her body was bruised and sore, but Edge seemed no more affected than if he'd spent a pleasant hour at the gym.

"You sure you want to see this?" Edge asked her once again. "It is probably going to be quite a bit messy in there."

"Yeah, I'm sure." She squeezed his hand, which was firmly clasped around hers and had been more often than not since they'd returned. "I'm curious."

"Me too, if you want the truth of it," he replied with a grin. "I have never really studied a Daemon up close without meaning to kill it as soon as possible. This should be educational if nothing else."

"There is that," she laughed.

He leaned reach down and caressed her bottom, then led her through the door of the interrogation room.

Tryton and The Traveler were seated before the Daemon, who appeared to be standing behind an odd shield, invisible but for the sparks that flew bright and wild whenever the beast dared to touch it. For once, The Traveler did not wear his cowl, and his long black hair shone with a dark, blood red sheen in the dim light of the room.

The effect The Traveler's face had on Edge was surprising. He gasped beside her, and his hand clenched hers in a grip grown suddenly fierce. "Grimm," he breathed.

The Traveler turned and stared at them from eyes as black as pitch and scarier besides. Bright points of light swam in their depths like glowing stars, hypnotic and entrancing even in the disturbing blackness. "At last we all know," was his dark response.

"What... How..." Edge was at a loss for words.

Tryton came forward. "Please. Sit, both of you. You are the last of your group to know Grimm's identity, Edge But no one outside your group knows. Please tell no one."

"But he died. He died a thousand years ago."

"Legends, Edge. That's all they are. Grimm was wounded in a great battle at the Gates, yes, but he did not die. He merely faded into the shadows, to work in secrecy and in stealth. He explored the lands of the Horde for many long years, but has come back to us at last."

"Why would he do that?" Edge looked from Tryton to the man in question. Emily was confused at the turn of events and merely looked on in silence.

Tryton turned and motioned towards the Daemon behind its invisible shield. "Because of that. Because of all of them. I knew, without finding and taking the source of their power—The Lord of the Horde himself—that these beasts would multiply and run rampant over the Earth." He sighed, and a thousand lifetimes of regrets lay dead in that sound. "So I sent my most trusted ally into enemy territory to find Lord of the Horde."

"A duty which I failed and unforgivably so," Grimm murmured.

"Not unforgivably," Tryton protested vehemently. "Never that. You have helped us in our fight far more than any other warrior, through your bravery and your cunning. You have failed at nothing."

"How can this be?" Edge interrupted. "You must be as old as Tryton, Traveler."

Grimm smiled. "Not so old in years. None would know the count of my years so well as he, though I admit I have long forgotten myself." It was clear the two warriors had been friends through many long ages.

"And the others know about you?"

"Yes," Grimm supplied, not one for many words even for explanation.

"When he saved Cady and Steffy it was futile to hide his identity from their mates, else how would they have trusted him so?" Tryton supplied.

"Then why let me know?" Edge asked, puzzled. "Why now?"

"Because I wanted you to know," Grimm answered, though his eyes rested firmly on Emily as he said them.

"And now that you have captured a Daemon—a feat no other besides yourself has ever accomplished in our history—everyone will surely guess at the truth," Tryton finished with a sigh.

"I wanted you and Emily to know before the rest," Grimm said emphatically. "You are my team, my family. You deserve to know firsthand who I am."

"I thank you, great warrior," Edge said with great deference, offering him a bow to which Grimm responded with a wry twist to his lips.

"What happened to your short words, Edge? I thought you distrusted all Travelers."

Edge chuckled. "Well, now that the pleasantries are over, I'm sure I'll get back to sniping at you whenever I can."

Tryton called their attention to the Daemon. "Now what to do about this devil, I wonder? It will not speak to us, except in its Horde tongue. Nor will it weaken."

The door opened. Cinder and Steffy joined them, neither of whom seemed surprised to find Grimm unmasked in their midst.

"Have you learned anything yet, Elder?" Steffy asked.

Tryton turned to Emily thoughtfully. "What say you, human? Do you think you can inspire it to speak?"

Frowning, she rose, leaving Edge and moving to stand before the Daemon. "I don't know," she finally answered to Tryton. "Before, they always spoke to me when we were fighting. Trying to surprise me into dropping my guard, I guess."

"Perhaps battle will draw it out," Cinder supplied.

Emily thought on it. "Why don't we let it out of this shield thing and find out?"

Tryton seemed reluctant but nodded to The Traveler. "Do it, Grimm. We'll see how this plays out."

The Daemon seemed to sense when the shield fell, with an innate cunning that had no doubt stood it well in the way of surviving. With a high-toned cry it leapt and fell upon Emily, no doubt seeking to Travel her out of the Shikar prison. Tryton's promises had been true. The wards of the Shikar world held and neither the Daemon nor Emily disappeared.

Emily rolled with the beast, seeking the dominant position, to hold it down and force it to speak. As expected the monster croaked in its hellish voice, unintelligible at first but with growing clarity.

"Emily, come," it said. "Emily, come."

Emily looked up at the stunned faces of those that surrounded her. Everyone had moved to flank her the minute the Daemon had struck, but now they appeared frozen in their tracks. "This is all I've heard them say," Emily told Tryton breathlessly.

"*Em-em. Em-em come pway wif me. Come,*" the Daemon gurgled in an unmistakably childish voice.

Emily screamed and launched herself off of the beast, shaking. "What did you say?" Immediately she reversed and grabbed the monster by the throat, straddling it once more. "What the fuck did you say?" she screamed down into its horrible face.

"Em-em, pway wif me. Em-em save me. Emily, save me!" It ended in a high scream.

Yelling in rage and fear and pain Emily beat down wildly into the monster's visage, crushing cartilage and bone with her blows. Edge came behind her and tried to pull her off, but she was too far gone in her emotion. "Damn you, motherfucker! Where did you hear that name?" She screamed and beat at the thing until it writhed in agony beneath her. Tryton moved in to help Edge, and it took the combined strength of the two Shikars simply to pull her off.

"What the Horde is wrong with you, Emily?" Edge shook her as she tried in vain to crawl back over the Daemon.

Emily was sobbing, crying and shouting hysterically. "Oh God. It called me Em-em. No one's called me Em-em but my little sister. It used her voice, *it used her voice —*"she cried.

"I didn't know you had a sister," Tryton said.

Grimm, who had immediately grabbed the wounded Daemon, went still, looking at her intently. He seemed most interested in her response, that much was clear in his stance, and even through her tears she could feel the burn of his black eyes upon her.

"I don't. She's dead," Emily sobbed. "She's been dead for *three years*. My poor Raine, oh my baby sister. How did this fucking monster know about her nickname for me? How could it know that?"

Steffy laid a cool hand on her shoulder. "Raine? You're Raine's Em-em?"

Emily looked up with dazed eyes. "What?"

"Your sister. She was Raine Lansing?"

"Yes." Raine hiccupped.

"Tall blonde, with pale blue eyes, and a crooked nose? Went to the Boston College of Music a few years ago?"

Emily grabbed her. "Yes! You knew her?"

Steffy gasped. "She was my best friend. My only friend," she cried. "She talked about you all the time!"

Everyone in the room was stunned by the news. In a night of surprising revelations, this one was the most unexpected.

"You knew her? You knew Raine before she died?"

Steffy nodded slowly. "I was there, where she had the accident. I wasn't allowed to see much, though. One of the paramedics was so affected by what she saw down in that ditch," Steffy shuddered, "I don't think the woman was ever the same again. There was blood from the road down into the trees, so I guess it was pretty bad nearer the car."

"I didn't see you." Emily swallowed hard. "At the funeral, I mean. Her body was lost somewhere in the snow. What was left of it after the initial impact was thrown clear of the car, but we had a service for her. I would have remembered you had I seen you."

Steffy's face shadowed with remembered pain. "I couldn't go. It was too hard to let go of Raine that way. Too final."

Emily nodded and turned to look at the Daemon, clutched tightly in Grimm's strong hands. "But how did that thing know to call me Em-em? How could it use her voice, from when she was just a little thing?"

Tryton and Edge pulled her to her feet. Edge held her steady against him, heart pounding in her ear.

"I don't know," Tryton murmured. "But I intend to find out."

Edge ushered Emily out of the room, giving the Daemon a wide berth in case she decided to launch herself at it again.

"How the plot doth thicken," murmured Grimm, as the door closed behind her.

Chapter Fifteen

Three days passed and still the Shikars learned nothing from their prisoner. After Emily had left, it had made no further move to speak of anything useful no matter how many tricks they tried to persuade it. Beyond a few threats spoken in garbled Horde-speak, there had been no further developments.

Cady's arm healed rapidly, her Shikar body repairing itself like magic. The day after her injury she was good as new, if a little pensive and quieter than usual. Obsidian doted on her, of course, seeing to her every whim and desire. Their son, Armand, sensed something was amiss and loved on his mother with extra care. The family had taken to their rooms, but for their routine evening meetings with Tryton.

Having taken care of their primary duty in securing a live Daemon, the team had taken the past few days off.

Emily stayed quiet in her room, thoughts troubled. She'd heard, of course, when their captive Daemon had died on the second day. It had succumbed, apparently of starvation, cut off as it was from its necessary psychic link to its overlord and unable to feed on fresh energy. Emily had been glad.

The beast had known about her sister. Somehow. It was too horrible to be borne.

The days passed in quiet solitude. Steffy had wanted to visit, perhaps to reminisce about Raine, but Emily had refused to see her. Had refused to see anyone. Even Edge.

Surprisingly, Edge had proven most understanding about her need for solitude. Though he came and knocked on her door every day, and collected her for their evening meetings, he never pressed the matter. Nor did he demand entry, as Emily had almost half suspected he might.

On the third night of seclusion, Emily fell into a troubled sleep—her first since the night of the Daemon capture. Almost immediately, an odd occurrence for her after so long without rest, she dreamed.

Out of the darkness, Raine walked towards her, looking tired but happy to see her. "Hey, Em. Missed you," she said. Her voice was rough, as if long unused, but still the same youthful melody it had always been.

Emily sobbed and embraced her sister. "I missed you too," she whispered. She pulled back suddenly, remembering their last conversation, when they'd argued over Raine's failing grades. Raine, of course, had laughed it all away, but Emily regretted that their last words together had been volatile ones. "I'm sorry for all those times we fought. I'm sorry for all those hurtful things I said the last time we spoke. I just wanted what was best for you, I wanted you to succeed at everything you chose."

Raine laughed, the husky sound echoing in the dream realm around them. "Silly Em-em. I know that. We had a tempestuous relationship, you and I." She reached up and rubbed the crook of her nose—a battle scar from when they'd been only children. Emily had sorely regretted breaking her sister's nose. It had been an accident, but she'd never forgiven herself. "The best sisters always do."

Emily embraced her once more, fighting back a storm of tears.

Finally, this time, it was Raine who pulled back. "Listen, sis. There's something I need to tell you," she looked around nervously, "before they know I'm gone."

"What?" Emily asked, thinking how real and detailed the dream was despite their nebulous, gray surroundings.

"You can be one of them, Em. A Shikar. If you want to."

"What are you talking about?" Emily laughed, despite the intensity of her sister's words and gaze.

"Don't laugh, listen..." Raine's voice murmured on into the dream and Emily took heed as best she could.

When she awoke in a tangle of sweat-drenched covers, Raine's words still ringing in her ears, she at last came to the decision she knew, in her heart, was inevitable and right.

She was a human. So much weaker and slower than any Shikar, unable to perform any of the magical feats that were so much an integral part of their nature. Cady and Steffy had both been human, and in the crossover from that state to Shikar they had taken on the qualities of a warrior caste as if born to them. Perhaps *she* could gain their strengths as well.

And beyond any of these reasons that swam in and out of her mind was the one most important of all. Her growing love for Edge. No matter how she looked at it, no matter how she tried to rationalize her intentions without her heart clouding up the matter, it all came back to Edge.

Emily knew he would be the love of her life. And selfishly, she wanted more than a human life span to revel in that miracle.

If only he could find it in his heart to forgive what she must do.

Emily only hoped she hadn't completely lost her mind, as well as her heart, for what she was about to do was the craziest thing she'd ever done in her life. And success hinged on someone that likely didn't even exist outside of her dreams. Raine.

* * * * *

Naked and wanting, Emily crawled over the sleeping form of her lover. He was, if it were possible, even more attractive in repose. Edge's face was a smooth contrast of strength and beauty, his body naked and golden in the shadows of the darkened bedroom. The rippling muscles of his chest rose and fell with every deep breath, and it was all she could do to keep from moaning her rising desire aloud.

But she mustn't wake him. Emily knew, without a doubt, that he'd never willingly agree to what she was about to attempt. Oh he'd agree to the sex, would he ever...but she meant to have him without any means of protection between them. There was no way Edge would agree to that. If she survived—*if*—Edge might be mad at her, would probably even rage at her since his temper was so unpredictable and volatile. But Emily trusted that he wouldn't hate her for it.

She prayed he wouldn't.

It was a risk. A dangerous one, considering how strongly she cared for him already, but one she had to take. She loved him—of course she loved him, how could she *not*—but she loved her world and her people too. And to protect her world in the best way, she must become a

Shikar. With all the Shikar gifts and strength, she would at last be able to serve her race in the way she'd always wanted to.

In doing this she would risk all — her life, Edge's love, and her very soul if he turned away from her. But if she won, the risks would have been worth it...so long as Edge still cared for her in the end.

And at last she would be able to make a true difference in the fight to save the world.

Careful not to wake him, she stealthily climbed over his body, pausing to kiss his splendorous form whenever the temptation became too great. His body was as eager as hers, even in sleep. The thick, long sword of his cock rose in salute, reaching well past his navel at full length. Golden as the rest of him, the sight of its thick shaft and mushroom head made her mouth water.

Pressing a soft, tentative kiss on his firm, round sac, she watched for any sign that he might wake. His flavor was a mixture of sandalwood and musky male essence and made her yearn for a deeper taste. She swirled her tongue over him, laving his testicles with kisses and licks until she could deny her urges no more.

Taking his cock firmly in hand, she guided her watering mouth over him. He was so big, so thick it was nearly impossible for her to take more than the great head of him past her lips. Sucking and licking him she took him as deep as she could, opening her mouth as wide as she could until he slipped deep into her throat.

Edge sighed and arched up into her mouth. Shooting her gaze upward she was relieved to see him still asleep, though now with a small smile playing about his lips.

Taking a risk she knew was folly, but unable to stop herself, she moved up and down upon him. Sucking him. Licking him. Kissing him. Until her own body was trembling with need, her pussy already flooded and tingling with anticipation.

If Edge still cared for her after this was all over, she would have to try this again someday. When there wasn't so much riding on the secrecy of her seduction, of course. It was magical, having him so quiet and still beneath her. So vulnerable, or at least appearing that way. She rather doubted Edge was ever really vulnerable, asleep or not.

Gently releasing him, though unable to resist suckling him one last time—like a flesh lollipop—she moved to straddle him at last.

"I love you, Edge. I do. Please forgive me." She breathed a kiss against his mouth as she sank down over his steely girth.

So wet was her body, so ready and aroused for his that his cock slipped easily into her. As if it belonged there, in the very heart of her. He filled her until her intimate skin was stretched taut to accommodate his great width. She sank down with a sigh, deeper and deeper until there was no space between their conjoined bodies. His flesh reached far into the depths of her; at this angle she was penetrated more fully than ever she had been before, and it was very nearly perfect.

It would have been, had he been awake. But she shied away from the guilt of her deception. Best not to dwell on it.

Emily began to move. Rotating her hips gently on his, thrusting her sheath up and down over his delicious cock until her breath hitched and deepened. Nearly mindless in her ever-growing desire, she moved more firmly and was far more careless than she should have been. Edge moaned and moved beneath her, rousing enough to feel her upon him.

"Emily," he breathed, hands moving to grip her hips as she rode him.

Fearing that with all his stamina, he would be able to stave off orgasm with time enough to fully waken and put a stop to all her scheming, Emily licked her index finger and reached beneath their softly rocking bodies. Hoping that Shikar men had sensitive prostates just as human men did, she gently slid her finger into his anus and ground her pelvis into him in an effort to help him find release the soonest.

Edge inhaled sharply and nearly bucked her off in reaction. He moaned. The sound choked off abruptly as he gritted his teeth, finally waking but too late to stop the inevitable. Eyes flying open in surprise, his body bucked twice more into hers. Emily came with a cry, the orgasm taking her by surprise. Her cunt tightened, twisting her body on a rack of ecstasy, and Edge met her with his own release.

So fast, she barely had time to come down from the pleasure of climax, her body turned to ice.

The floor rose to meet her as she toppled bonelessly off his body and bed, and Edge's howl of anguish echoed in her ears a moment before darkness and silence took her deep.

Chapter Sixteen

"Grimm."

He started out of the doze, which had lulled him in the dark. It had been the first sleep he'd had in three days — since Emily had revealed her tie to Raine.

Emily wasn't the only one who suffered from chronic insomnia.

"*Grimm*," the whispery voice came again, though there was no one in the room. The voice was in his mind.

"I hear you," he murmured, closing his eyes and fading into the realm of limbo where he knew *she* was waiting.

Raine's weary gaze was both a balm and a cutting knife deep in his aching soul. "You haven't much time," she said in way of greeting. "She's already fading."

And he knew. Holy Horde he knew, without having to ask, why she'd brought him here. "Emily," he whispered.

As Raine had protected her friend Steffy so too would she protect her sister, even in death. "I can't hold her for long. Her will is as strong in death as it is in life. It wants to leave this place, to travel on. You must go to them. You must save her."

"But she cannot cross over," he warned her. "She has not the gifts or the strength."

Raine smiled. "I have given her what gifts and strength she needs. But you must meet her half way, as you did the others. Her life depends on you now."

How could she sound so certain, this woman who was human and yet possibly so much more? How could she know their secrets? Even in death she was psychically strong. She must be, to know so much. To call him here to this in-between place. Grimm felt the loss of her that much more, seeing her here again after thinking on her for so long.

"Go now. I'll be waiting for you with her," she said. "Hurry."

He reached for her, wanting to touch her. More than anything he wanted to touch her, to see if she was as real as she seemed. But a feeling like no other he'd ever experienced in all his long years swept over him before he could manage it. The force of a thousand hands pressed in on him, a power equal or greater even than his own, pushing him through the veil and back into his own world. Raine had thrown him back, to hurry him on his way.

Grimm was stunned. The woman had dared to exert her power over him and it was strong, stronger than any other he'd encountered. Dead and trapped between worlds though she may be, Raine was indeed formidable.

Opening his eyes, once again in his own world, in his own chamber, he was surprised to find a mist of tears had filled his eyes and spilled down over his cheeks. "*But O! as to embrace me she inclined, I waked, she fled, and day brought back my night.*" He quoted his favorite Milton in a gruff whisper.

Gathering his composure once again, Grimm brushed his thoughts aside and Traveled. He would try against hope to save Emily. Though he feared he would fail, he would try.

For Raine.

Chapter Seventeen

Edge rolled off the bed after her, grabbing her to him as she collapsed.

"Let me have her." Grimm's voice was startling, and he loosened his hold instinctively as The Traveler pulled Emily from him.

He looked into Grimm's face, in pain and grief and anger. Anger at Emily for what she'd done. Anger at himself for not seeing it would happen, sooner or later. "I didn't mean to," he offered helplessly.

"She *did*," Grimm said simply. Raising Emily's hand to his mouth, he bit down.

Edge gasped and moved to stop him.

Grimm looked at him, halting him with but the force of his gaze. "I have to. Her blood carries the signature of her very spirit. I must know the scent and taste of her on the other side, or I will lose her."

Satisfied with the answer he hadn't expected from the quiet Traveler, Edge subsided and watched the scene unfold with worry and horror. "Can you save her?" he asked, hoping against hope for what he feared was an impossibility.

"I don't know. But I'm going to try." With that promise Grimm disappeared, leaving Edge to grab for Emily's body, lest she fall with a bump once more onto the floor.

* * * * *

"Hang on, Emily. Hang on to me."

Emily could feel her sister clutching tightly, holding her close...though she had no body to feel with. It was more a sensation, a knowledge in her mind that Raine was holding her fast, keeping her safe.

She could not speak. Could not see. Could not feel. She could only hear — or perhaps *sense* — Raine's voice in her mind. If indeed she had a mind in this place. If this was a place at all...she didn't know.

She was losing all sense of self.

Who am I?

"You're Emily. My own Em-em, my sister. Stay with me. Hang on."

Who are you?

"Hang on. Just hang on to me, please."

The urge to float away, to fade into nothingness was all she knew. But hands clutched her — what were hands? — and a voice called out to her, keeping her trapped when all she wanted to do was...

Die.

Emily felt her soul wrench as the thought became clearer. No. She did not want to die. She must fight against the lure of oblivion.

"That's it, big sis. Fight it. You'll be home soon."

Home. Where was home? *With Edge*, the tiny thought drifted, but was strong. Like the voice of her sister was strong. The voice of Raine.

"You're drifting in and out of life and death. Don't be scared. But hang on to me. Don't go..." The mantra was continued, over and over, until Emily heard two voices crooning it to her. One was Raine's.

The other was…

"It is I, Grimm. Come back with me, Emily, if you want to live."

I do. I do want to live, she tried to call out, but she had no voice with which to scream.

"It's all right. I've got you." Grimm's spirit was like a warm, safe blanket that surrounded and covered her. Giving her shelter, guiding her back. Back. To life.

As though through a vast, growing distance she heard Raine call out, though not to her this time. To Grimm.

"You remember I told you once that you remind me of someone?" she called.

"I do. I remember everything you ever said," he murmured.

"You reminded me of the Grim Reaper, " Raine laughed. "It was your cowl, you see. And your sad presence here." Raine's voice was fading. Emily's ears filled with a rush, like supersonic booms that grew louder and louder.

"Don't be so sad, Traveler," came the last of Raine's shouted words. "And take care of my sister!"

The incorporeal world closed like a tunnel around them — she could almost see it, though she had not sight. The real world rushed in on Emily with the force of a thousand one-ton bricks. She choked on air, her body trapped her spirit and held fast to it. She screamed.

And awoke to a new life.

Chapter Eighteen

Emily looked into the mirror at her black, Traveler eyes, hardly believing what she saw reflected there. Behind her, the entire team was assembled, discussing the miracle of her escape from death.

Edge was silent. She knew he was angry. Far angrier than she could have guessed he would be.

But she did not regret her decision. She could not regret it. She had survived, after all.

The minute she'd regained consciousness, Tryton had appeared, railing at her for her folly. She'd barely had time to cover her nudity before Obsidian and the others had come, knowing already what had happened through whatever pipeline that supplied them with all their other secret knowledge. But Edge had said not one word to her, or to anyone. He left all the explaining to her.

"Who is this woman, Raine, that she knows so much about us?" Tryton demanded. "And why have you kept your knowledge of her secret, Traveler?"

"She is no threat to us, Elder. She is dead," Grimm said tightly.

"But not so far gone to the living world that she cannot help Steffy and Emily," The Elder fumed. "I hate the puzzle of her. I hate not knowing who she is or how she can do what she does."

"Well, be grateful, Tryton," Steffy interjected with no small amount of bristling anger on Raine's behalf. "If it weren't for her both Emily and I would be dead by now. And while you might not have mourned the loss of two humans, I can promise you would have missed us as Shikar warriors."

Tryton winced, a wounded look making him look older than normal. "Do you really think that? That I wouldn't have cared had you died? Of course I am grateful to Raine's Shade. You are all like my children, and my truest friends. It would have crippled me if either of you had died."

"Strategically, you mean. Because you need all the fighters you can get," Steffy muttered testily.

"Hold your tongue," Cinder commanded sharply Steffy gasped before he soothed away the sting of his words by pulling her close. "We're all too emotional now We should not say things in anger or hurt that we do not mean."

Emily turned back to them. "I did what I did because I had to. And I knew that I would be safe. Raine told me I would be all right."

"In a dream. A dream that could have been only that." Edge spoke at last, anger tightening his every muscle into stone.

"But it wasn't just a dream. It was real."

"You didn't know that!" he shouted.

Taking his punishing words as her due, she subsided Silence reigned for several moments before Edge spoke again, more calmly this time. "You should have at least discussed this with me first."

"You would never have agreed," she sighed.

Edge shot to his feet. "Of course I wouldn't have! There was every possibility that you would die," he bit out.

"Calm down, Edge. She didn't die." Cady tried to soothe him. "That's the most important thing to remember right now."

Running his fingers through his hair in frustration, Edge sat back down and fell into an angry, brooding silence once again.

Tryton moved to Emily and lifted her chin up, to better study her face. "A Traveler. A rare Caste, even for a full-blood Shikar."

"Raine shared herself with me. I," she swallowed under his heavy gaze, "I never even guessed she was psychic. I never would have believed it had she told me."

"She told you this? She told you what her gifts were?" he asked quizzically.

It was Grimm, surprisingly, who answered for her. "Astral projection. That was her gift, was it not?"

Emily nodded, grateful when Tryton turned from her to The Traveler. "Yes. She said she'd been doing it since she was a little girl. But she never told me until tonight. She was afraid I wouldn't believe her. And she was right— I was too cynical to ever have believed such a claim. As it is now, I still find it hard to believe. But for this." She reached up to touch the area beneath her new eyes, but let her hands fall to her side as the full weight of what they signified hit her.

"I'm truly a Shikar now," she said in wonder.

"Yes," Tryton answered. "Though you could have stayed human and we would have loved and kept you all the same, you are now truly one of us. It cannot be undone," he said warningly.

"I wouldn't want to undo it," she said firmly and it was the truth. "And now that I'm as strong as you, I can do what must be done to fight the Daemons."

Tryton grunted. "And what is that?"

"Meet them at the Gates. On their own ground. We must invade."

The entire group gasped, though Edge seemed most intent on what she had to say and held his silence.

"Invasion is folly," Obsidian bit out.

"To meet the Daemons on their own soiled ground would end in a bloodbath of fallen warriors," Cinder said at the same time.

Emily shook her head. "No. Raine knows their weakness. The Daemons search for a way to live above ground. They need the power that their feedings will supply them with as their numbers grow."

"So the Lord of the Horde makes a new army then," Tryton said brokenly, shoulders slumped.

"Not Lord Daemon, no," Emily continued. "Daemon is missing, his power sustaining them withdrawn. The monsters make their own army now, with their own power — stolen from the flesh of the living."

"How can Raine know all of this?" Tryton demanded once again.

"She just does, all right? And she says we must meet the Daemon threat head on. At the Gates to their own world. With the full force of our army."

"And lose what warriors we have, on the promises given by a Shade that we wage an open war with our enemies?" Tryton scoffed. "No."

"Yes." Edge spoke and all eyes turned to him. "It makes sense. We've never attempted such a charge. The Horde would never suspect it." His gaze moved to Emily's, and though there was still anger within their depth, they also softened in hope at the prospect of victory in such a battle.

"Edge is right," Grimm agreed. "And I trust to Raine in this."

Tryton gritted his teeth. "Would you trust her with your life?"

"Yes," Grimm answered without hesitation.

Tryton sighed, a long and weary sound. "I will confer with the Council. I cannot launch a strike without their full support."

"I will go with you," Obsidian said at once, rising from his seat. "I, too, have faith in the Shade's plan."

"So do I," Steffy added.

"Me, too. *Duh.* She sure as hell seems to know a lot more than we do about all this crazy shit that's been happening," Cady quipped.

Everyone stood now and gathered to leave, Edge among them, though Tryton motioned him and Emily back. "You two have much to discuss. We will persuade the Council to see as we do in this matter."

"So you support us then, Elder?" Emily asked, trying to ignore the nervous thrill of apprehension that swamped her at the idea of being with Edge alone so soon.

Tryton smiled. "I supported it from the beginning, of course. I was just testing you all with my show of hesitance, to make sure you knew for yourselves that this was the path we must take."

The scary thing was, Emily didn't know if he was joking or not.

The group left as silently as it had come, leaving her alone with a very angry, very volatile Edge. The silence stretched out, heavy and strained, between them. Emily was at a loss, not knowing what to say. She wanted him to forgive her...but she couldn't apologize for what she'd done.

"I should beat you," he said at last, heavily. His head and shoulders slumped.

She bristled. "I wouldn't let you."

"As if you could stop me," he replied with heady challenge, head whipping back up to face her.

"I don't want to fight with you, Edge." She tried a different approach. "I know what I did was wrong. I know it scared you—"

"Scared? Me? Now why do you think I would be scared—you only died in my arms. What's to be scared of about that?" he bit out.

Emily took a deep breath, when what she really wanted to do was snap back at him. But she was learning more and more about Edge, and it was clear to her by now that he used anger as a shield when his deeper emotions were too powerful for him to understand. "I know it scared you, because you love me," she said softly.

Edge closed his eyes and turned away. "How could I love a woman who would put her life in danger, and use me as an instrument in the doing?"

She swallowed, his words cutting her deep. "I had to do it, Edge. For myself, for my sister. For the world. And for you."

He turned back to her, eyes suspiciously damp. "For me? How can you think I would want you to take such a risk?"

"I know you wouldn't, that's why I took it upon myself. The choice was mine, and if I died you would have had a clear conscience."

Edge pursed his lips and looked away. "I would have felt guilt. It would have killed me...had you not come back it would have killed me too."

Swallowing, crying and unable to halt her tears, she reached out for him. "I had to do it. You and I could have never had a life together. My years are short to your kind—you said so yourself. I wanted a Shikar's lifetime with you. I love you, Edge. I do."

Edge pulled her tightly to him, fisting his hand in her hair, burying his face in it as he too began to weep. "I could have lost you. Damn you for a stubborn fool, but I could have lost you forever. What good would that have done either of us?" He pressed fervent kisses to her hair, her temples, her face.

"I'm sorry. For scaring you and for hurting you, I'm sorry. But I'm glad I did it," she cried.

Pulling back, he looked deep into her eyes. "I'll miss the blue. My Emily blue. But I'm so glad you're all right. It's worth the loss."

Emily sniffed and smiled. "I'm glad. I'll miss them too. But if I can do a fraction of the things you Shikars can do then I'll be happy. And so long as I have you. Do I have you?"

"You do. You know it. From that first night in the alley, when you told me to freeze, I knew I was a goner. You should have too."

"Kiss me. Kiss me until you love me as much as I love you," she whispered even as his mouth descended on hers.

"It's too late. It's already too late," he said over and over, with each kiss.

His mouth moved over her face, down to her throat and neck. Nuzzling her, kissing and nibbling her sensitive skin until she moaned. His hands pushed aside the robe she wore—his robe—which he'd given her to hide her nudity in front of Tryton. It fell away, exposing her fully to his gaze.

"I've wanted this so much for the past three days," he breathed.

"Me too," she admitted.

"Don't ever keep yourself from me again."

"I won't, I swear it."

The dark auburn of his hair glistened in the light as he bent his head to her breast. Emily saw her nipple disappear into the seam of his lips. He pulled her into his mouth, using his tongue and teeth to pull and twist delicately. It popped out, shining wet when he was through. "Like a peach," he murmured before moving on to the other. "I have always loved peaches."

Emily's head fell back as he fed on her, mouth scorching her nipples and chest. His arm supported her around the waist, holding her up for his pleasure when she would have swooned backward in ecstasy.

"I was asleep the last time. I feel a mighty need to make up for that slight," he promised darkly, claiming her mouth once again for a heady, soul-searching kiss.

"I'm sorry," she said, and he quieted her with a finger to her lips.

"Let us speak of it no more."

He bent down and hooked an arm beneath her knees. Swooping her up into his arms, he carried her—raining kisses upon her swollen lips with every step—into his bedroom. He deposited her gently onto the mattress, before pulling away. "Stay right there. I have a gift for you."

He left the room but was back before she had a chance to miss him. He held out his hand, offering her the gift that waited within it.

"My goodness. It's beautiful." A tiny wooden charm hung suspended from a long, delicate crystal chain. It was a lifelike carving of two serpentine dragons entwined in a mating embrace that formed the shape of a heart. "It's absolutely beautiful," she breathed.

Edge leaned forward and fastened the chain around her neck. "I made it while you were in seclusion. I missed you so, I wanted you to have a piece of me with you always."

"Oh, baby." She smiled around new tears. "You're always with me wherever I go, even without this lovely gift. Thank you. I'll never take it off," she promised.

Then there was no more time for words between them. Within seconds Edge was as nude as she, and his body was hot and heavy atop hers. His hands and lips and hair were everywhere upon her, burning her, tickling her, making her moan and cry out. He paid special attention to the tender flesh behind her knees once he realized how erotic she found the attention. He licked and kissed her there, until she was keening and begging him for more. Always more.

And more he gave her until she could take no more.

The broad strength of his hands turned her over effortlessly in the bed. His mouth fell immediately upon her rump, savoring the plump womanly flesh of her there. He licked his finger and tenderly slipped it into her anus for a few precious minutes, as she'd done earlier with him and she cried out with the immense pleasure it gave her.

He crawled up over her. So big and so strong he dwarfed her. Raising her up with one hand, he guided his cock to her rear with the other. Wetting himself in the plentiful juices of her pussy, he moved into position and slipped delicately into the tight portal of her ass.

"Oh God," she gasped in pleasure and in pain. But after an initial sting of discomfort the head of his cock slipped in and he rested there, heavy inside of her trembling body.

After letting her grow accustomed to the slight penetration, he moved deeper into her, slowly and gently until he was seated halfway inside her body. He growled and dug his fingers into the cheeks of her bottom. "You're so fucking tight, love. I think I'm going to die right here." He sounded as if it were the best idea he'd ever had.

Emily moved tentatively beneath him and they both gasped in pleasure. His hand reached between their bodies and stroked the silky skin of her cunt, paying special attention to the lips and clitoris. She shuddered and took him more fully into herself as her body yawned in preparation for release. "Oh Edge, I'm coming," she gasped in surprise and tormented delight.

Edge began slowly thrusting his fingers into her pussy, and his cock into her ass. He groaned raggedly in a language she should not have known, but did all the same, thanks to her newfound Shikar abilities. "You are so fucking sexy. Come for me baby, swallow me up."

As if on cue, her body clamped down on his, causing them both to cry out. Emily's cry turned into a scream as her body trembled and throbbed beneath his. He slid to the hilt inside of her. Three of his fingers filled her pussy to the knuckle, scraping her G-spot masterfully. She exploded, coming completely undone so that her orgasm poured over his hand and down between her legs.

The roar of a well-satisfied male sounded in her ear. Edge thrust hard and filled her with his ejaculate, his balls slapping her, his cock pulsing in the tight glove of her rear. Gasping, heart pounding loud enough for them both to hear, he collapsed upon her.

They rested, arms and legs entwined, until they at last found calm once more.

"I've only got one question."

"What's that?" His hand petted her from nape to rump, hypnotically.

"What the hell is the *Mone*?"

Edge laughed. "*Mone* as in the sex aid, *Mone*?" She nodded and he laughed again. "I will show you."

Chapter Nineteen

Both Edge and the *Mone* filled her pussy full to bursting. The *Mone* was wonderful, Emily had to admit. The sex toy was made of a clear, flexible material not unlike plastic. It was about the diameter of a disposable ink pen and several feet long. One end was slipped into the woman's anus or pussy; the other was a balloon that could be filled with warm water—as it was now—or some other liquid. The balloon was meant to be squeezed, so that as two lovers mated, the *Mone* gave tiny jettisons of liquid into the woman, easing the lovers' way and massaging them both as they thrust in unison.

Edge had Emily lying on the rim of the sunken tub in his bathroom. His legs were in the water of the bathtub but his body lie over hers, thrusting. Both his cock and the *Mone* reached deep within her, to the very heart of her until they were as one.

Clutching him to her, Emily wrapped her legs around his pumping hips, drawing him ever closer. Her nails raked down his back, until he hissed and bucked harder into the cradle of her thighs. Her clit burned and swelled as he rubbed against it with each motion, and she cried out in short, panting sobs for more and more…and more.

But just before she found the release she so desperately craved, Edge pulled out of her and moved down into the tub so that his head was between her thighs. His mouth was almost cool on her after the intensity of their loving, but it was silky smooth and wet and she gasped at the shock of it.

His lips wrapped around her clit and suckled. The long length of his tongue rimmed her every nook and cranny, exploring every fold until she was glistening wet from her juices, the *Mone's*, and his kiss. He delved deep into the core of her, sucking her nectar and coaxing forth more. Emily screamed and bowed up off the floor, knees spread wide as he rooted in her.

But just as before, when she was on the precipice of her climax, Edge pulled away. He climbed up over her body with a wicked smile and thrust deep, *hard*, into her.

"Time for your punishment, love." He kissed her sweat-dampened brow with a kiss that was deceptively gentle after his words.

"*What?*" she squeaked.

He lifted his head back to look at her, rotating his hips against her, moving inside of her until she moaned. "You heard me," he said once she'd quieted. "You need to be punished, if only a little, for the terror you caused me when you almost died."

And he was as good as his word. Thrusting over and over inside of her, using his fingers to pluck first at her nipples then at her clit, he played her body until she was at the very edge of release.

Only to pull back and effectively halt her flight into that sweet oblivion.

Orgasm after orgasm he staved off, never allowing her to rest or to find surcease from the wicked claws of his erotic dominion. The *Mone* was soon removed, for it would have given her the relief she craved had he not. His mouth and tongue filled her. His fingers and cock stretched her. In a storm of passion she raged at him begged him, pleaded and threatened...but he'd promised punishment and punishment is what he gave.

Unable to find release, her body became ultra sensitive to Edge's every touch. To his every kiss. After three hours of torment, even his breath had the power to make her scream as it played over the wet, swollen flesh o her pussy. And still there was no quarter given.

The most surprising thing to her, at least it was before she lost most of her ability to think, was that Edge delayed his own orgasm as well. As if he was punishing himself a much as her. A lucky thing for him it was, though. It was the only thing about the whole affair that kept her from raging at him.

Edge produced devices he called nippers, which he fastened to her aching, pouting nipples. A long leather dildo, the exact shape and size as he—no doubt made from a mold of his cock—was well lubricated and slipped gently into her anus. Turning and laying over her, he buried his face into her pussy and simultaneously slipped his cock into her mouth.

The taste of her own pussy was sticky sweet on him a he slid down her throat. The smell of him was heady, like sandalwood and rainwater in her nostrils. She breathed him deep and suckled, desperate for any piece of him to tease and torment as he visited her exquisite punishmen to every cell of her body.

He pulled away with a shout and a moan. "No more. can take no more," was his hoarse cry as he turned again and thrust, balls deep, into her cunt.

He thrust hard and deep, biting and sucking her breasts as she raked her nails down his shoulders and back. "I sought to punish you," he said around a mouthful of swollen nipple, "but I fear I have suffered far more than you."

The violent force of his thrusts had her body arching up off the floor. Water splashed everywhere. Their bodies slipped and slid in the puddles that surrounded them. And this time...oh this wondrous time...when she climbed that peak to blessed climax he let her fly and joined her.

Chapter Twenty

"We ready this night for battle. Some of us—many o us—may not return. But fight we must and in this way, i we hope to gain any ground in the invasion our enemie have already begun. Fear not, for we are strong together And though we may die, our fight will never have been i vain. Our legacy is the survival of our children. Of thos who live on Earth, oblivious to the struggle, bu endangered most grievously by the threat it poses shoul we lose. And of the warriors who will live to rejoice i victory when the fighting is done. We go now to war Long live the Alliance!"

Tryton's speech was met with the cheers of a hundre Shikar warriors. Emily felt Edge's strong hand clasp her warmly. "I love you," she mouthed to him over the din.

He mouthed the words back with a wink and a smile.

Groups of Shikars gathered around a dozen or s Travelers. Emily, untrained as such, went with her grou to Grimm, who waited in silence with his customary blac cowl obscuring his features. Cinder smiled at her an teased, "Let's hope this sister of yours knows what she' talking about."

Emily had no doubts. "She does."

The Traveler nodded and took them to the Gates.

Once she'd regained her wits after the dizzying trip Emily studied their surroundings with an eye for ever possible detail. The air was indeed foul here, as Edge ha warned her it would be. It smelled of brimstone and old death. Hot and sulfurous, every breath held the taint of the Daemons' world.

If the Christians' Hell were a physical place, it would undoubtedly look something like this.

The landscape was a study of black, crimson, and orange rock, of hills and crevices covered in naught but barren terrain. No living thing grew here; no vegetation could have survived the harsh environs. It was hot and sticky and there was no breeze to give relief.

Everything looked rough and sharp. Not even the rocks were smooth. Emily had once seen pictures of an angry and active volcano in Hawaii, and the rocks on the ground seemed eerily similar, pitted and brittle as they were. Needle-sharp stalagmites jutted out from the ground here and there, giving the earth its own unique set of dangerous looking teeth.

The sky was black; the clouds were low and heavy and tinged with red so that they looked full of blood. There was no sun. No celestial satellite to grace the sky. This place existed beyond Emily's notion of space, of the universe. It was clear for all to see that this place existed somewhere else altogether. Someplace...*other*.

If this land had ever been anything but wholly evil, utterly tainted, Emily could not see it. The barren waste stretched on for miles in all directions but one—where a veil separated the Shikar world from this one—and she realized that though the Shikars called this place the Gates, there were no actual gates to be seen. Because there were no gates, beyond that separating veil. This *world* was the Gates. It was a different dimension, an entire world unto itself that lived on the edges of reality. On the edges of sanity.

It was the perfect place for the Daemons to call home.

A group of Shikars carried a large horn, several fee long onto the ground and curved like the tusk of a mammoth. One of the warriors blew into it and it sounded long and loud, its echo reached to the farthest corners of the Gates. A clarion call to the Daemons who no doubt lay in wait for their chance to strike.

"Get ready, love," Edge warned her.

And none too soon, for it was then that a hundred — no, perhaps five times that to Emily's thinking — Traveled into their midst with no warning. The war had begun at last.

The ring of battle was loud and echoing as a drumbeat in the still air. Daemon after Daemon fell, only to be replaced by more. Still more. Countless more. Until the Shikars were grossly outnumbered. Who could have guessed, who could have *dreamed*, that so many of the beasts existed? It was chaos and it was hell, but the Shikars fought with the skill of the centuries in their every move and their losses were blessedly few as the Daemons were cut down before their might and strength.

Shaking herself from the shock of seeing it all, Emily moved and engaged the nearest Daemon. Unprepared for the strength she now had at her disposal, the punch she intended to throw went straight through the chest cavity of the beast. Gritting her teeth she shoved the monster back, taking its heart in her fist as her hand passed back through its center. Crushing it to a pulp effortlessly, she moved on, reveling in her newfound strength.

Out of the corner of her eye, Emily saw Edge twirl blades winking like a propeller of razor-sharp knives as he spun. Daemons fell in pieces at his feet. Throwing out hi hands, blades shot from his wrists and flew into the air, traveling through the fray of battle, dodging Shikars but slicing with deadly intent through any Daemons that chanced stepping in their way. They had a mind of their own, or Edge commanded their flight, Emily didn't know which, but it was an impressive sight.

They came back to him, slipping back into the flesh of his wrists. All without causing him or any Shikar the slightest harm.

A Daemon's hand slammed down onto her shoulder, and she jerked. So strong was she now, that her reflexive move tore the beast's arm from its body. Wasting precious little time for surprise, she punched out its heart and turned to engage another. And another. She lost count of just how many, but was thankful that it didn't seem to matter anymore. Her Shikar body had yet to slow or tire.

Whatever had made the Daemons show her mercy as a human was gone now that she had changed. They fought her with as much deadly intent as they did any other Shikar. It was puzzling, but then she'd never understood why they had spared her the brunt of their brutality in the first place. Perhaps it was a secret she would never know.

A group of a dozen or so monsters moved to flank her. Her steps faltered and she was forced to retreat as they stalked forward, moving as one unit. Emily kicked out at the nearest one, satisfied to hear the crunch of bone as her opponent fell. She knew it would be seconds and no more before the beast regained its feet, but it felt good to at least injure it all the same.

They were upon her and closing in fast. She had nowhere to go but backwards, and then even that was lost to her as she backed straight into an outcropping of stalagmite. With a mighty cry the group jumped her en masse. Emily steeled herself for the impact of a dozen bodies, each intent on ripping her apart in a rage.

Before her wide eyes, the Daemons halted in mid lunge. Their skin bubbled and blistered. They screamed in fear and pain. Shuddering, even as they died they reached for her, every pore of their flesh opened and wept. Blood and muck separated from the beasts' forms—the very liquids of their bodies separating from the solids—leaving only dried husks that held their empty shape behind. Round droplets of those fluids hovered and glistened in the air, then fell to the ground. The Daemon husks shivered then they, too, fell and shattered to dust on the ground.

"Be more careful, young Traveler," Tryton warned her, for it had been he who had saved her with such ease. Even after such a raw display of power he was unruffled and calm as always.

Barely given the time to thank him, he was gone, back into the thick of the battle. And Emily was moved to do the same, despite her close call. Her new family and friends needed her. She would fight at their side until this business was done, come what may. Having made it this far, she was determined to see it through to the end.

But suddenly, all Daemon movement stopped.

Frozen, unmoving, the Daemons appeared trapped by some unseen force. All of them, over the far plains of the battlefield, ceased to move completely.

As if beckoned, Emily shifted her gaze upward to the horizon. There, in the distance, two lone men stood, their cloaks billowing on a breeze that was not there. One of the men, the taller of the two, raised his hand as if in greeting...but it proved not so innocent a gesture.

Every Daemon cried out in pain and terror...then was silenced just as swiftly as they'd been frozen. With a wave of his hand the man smote the army, rendering it to dust upon the barren, rocky ground. From half a mile away, without putting a finger on the beasts, he managed to do what a hundred Shikar could not, and in mere seconds. This mighty army of the Horde was decimated, the fighting was ended.

As quickly as they had appeared, the men turned and were gone, leaving no trace of their identity behind. It was as if they had never been.

The battle was over.

Epilogue
One week later…

"I love you, mate. I love everything about you. I love the way you smell, the way you taste, the way you feel." Edge growled against the crook of her shoulder and neck. "I could eat you all up."

Emily giggled happily, and was unashamed at the sound.

"Promises, promises," she goaded in husky invitation.

"I'll show you I'm a man of my word, woman!" He pounced upon her, spreading her legs wide with his hand and covering her pussy with his mouth.

She squealed in surprise…then moaned.

And he did indeed eat her all up.

* * * * *

Cinder's skin burned into Steffy's. His clenching fists left scorch marks in the bedding beside her head.

"Levine is gonna be pissed when we order new sheets. That's the third time this month she's had to make us new ones." Steffy moaned as her husband thrust his wide, long cock into the depths of her warm, willing body.

"Then we'll go to the surface and buy a decent supply there instead," he groaned. His tongue laved the shell of her ear, his breath as hot as the rest of him.

His hips rocked on hers, bearing her down into the mattress.

She came with a scream

* * * * *

Cady gasped at the feel of Sid's cock as it slid deep into her ass.

"I love you, Cady. So much," he whispered into her ear.

"I love you too," she moaned, riding wave after wave of pleasure. "Now shut up and do me." She laughed.

"As my lady wishes," Obsidian promised before increasing the tempo and strength of his thrusting hips.

From a dark corner of the room, Grimm's eyes burned as he witnessed their loving. His hand stroked the powerful jut of his cock as he timed his pleasure's peak to theirs. Though the lovers entwined on the bed performed for his benefit as much as their own, it was a golden-haired angel he saw in his mind's eye as he came in a heated flood onto his hand.

The room reeked of sex. It smelled of love, an eternity's worth and more.

It gave him solace, where before there had been only sadness and regret.

* * * * *

Far away from the loving couples, far away even from the land of the Shikar, and Daemons, Tryton sat upon the Louvre's rooftop in Paris, France.

His thoughts were somewhat bleak with the pain o best-forgotten memories and the longing of an immortal': loneliness. Though the battle was done, the war was fa from over. The Horde had lost the bulk of their numbers but they would rise again. They always did, like a plague.

Before it was done many would die, on both sides Tryton knew it. All the Shikar knew and accepted it. Bu the Shikar Alliance had stood for many centuries agains their foe and they would continue to do so until the las warrior was standing.

Though who would win remained uncertain, Trytor was beginning to have some hope that it was the Alliance who would triumph over the threat of evil.

More than anything the two figures on the horizon, ir the bleak land of the Gates, had given him that hope. He wanted his suspicions about them to be true, despite the odds that were stacked against such an impossibility. They had helped the Shikars, after all, so was it total folly to see them as possible allies?

He hoped not.

Tryton put on a pair of dark black sunglasses and leapt off of the building's rooftop, soaring in the wind like a bird. And as the rays of a new dawn streaked out ove. the horizon, he struck out for the nearest shore. The sur warmed his face and skin...but it did not burn. Its golder glow felt like an old friend welcoming him home after too long an absence. This was the world the Shikar had left sc long ago. This was the world he wanted to save.

This was the world he vowed one day to return to.

In the warmth of the sun, in the air and finally in the sea, Tryton found hope and was glad.

Enjoy this excerpt from:

MANACONDA
SACRED EDEN
THE HORDE WARS 4

"I think that, for once, I am actually looking forward to this visit to the surface world," Sid admitted to his wife.

"Well, now that the Daemons are reduced to nothing more than a handful of stragglers, I can see why. Without them to worry about, it'll be a field trip for us instead of a battle," Cady chuckled.

"This is true. But long before the Daemons began escaping into the world of humans, it was rare that I had any true interest in visiting there."

"But that was before you had me to take you to all the fun and happening places up there," Cady teased, buckling her Sig-Sauer 9mm P-226 pistol to her black-clad thigh. Though she didn't expect any danger tonight—it had been almost a year since the last Daemon attack after all—it never hurt to be prepared. The long skirt of her reverend-style overcoat would hide any evidence of the weapon should she garner too many curious stares…she hoped. But no way was she leaving her new favorite weapon behind.

"Baby," he chided, "I have my doubts that you even know of one such place. Before you became one of us, all your days and nights were spent working and fighting Daemons. You had no time for such idle pursuits as fun."

"Ooh, that was cold. I should spank you for that one," Cady mock-pouted, knowing that his words were true.

"Not before I spank you first," he quipped back with an exaggerated leer.

Pulling his long, black hair into a ponytail at his nape and securing it with a strip of rawhide, Sid strode over to an intricately carved wooden side-table that stood by the door. Cady couldn't help but admire the play of his roped muscles beneath the tight material of his black clothing. His tight, black, sexy clothing.

Tonight they wore no armor, as they might have but a year before when evil Daemons ran rampant over the earth. But they both preferred wearing dark colors so as to blend in with the night as they roamed above. Old habits died hard, it seemed, despite the lack of danger.

And they had to roam at night after all—Shikars were ultra-sensitive to the sunlight. Their race had dwelled in darkness for so long—thousands of years—that tolerance for the bright rays of daylight had been bred right out of them And though Cady had once been human herself—turned Shikar only by the powerful magic in the semen of her husband—she had not yet tested the theory that she might still be able to walk in the light.

She wasn't afraid of the risk, not really. But Obsidian had forbidden her to even think of testing the resilience of her flesh in the rays of the sun. While she wasn't always inclined to willingly heed a command that her beloved—yet arrogant—husband gave her, she had seen the stark fear in his eyes as he worried over the possibility of her injury, or even death. So she had, for once, decided to let her dearest have his way.

Giving up the sun was such a small price to pay for this new life she'd gained. A loving husband, a perfect son, the power to create fire with her mind and her will, and the ability to shoot deadly, poisonous blades from her flesh—without any real pain or effort—were huge boons that made the loss of daylight seem almost insignificant in comparison.

"I almost forgot, Desondra brought this when she came for Armand." Sid's deep, sexy voice snapped Cady out of her wandering thoughts.

She reached for the piece of folded parchment he held out for her. "Ah." She nodded when she realized what it was. "I'd meant to ask you about this earlier."

It was the main reason they were going up to the surface world, this piece of parchment. Or rather, what was written on it.

"Let's see…Edge wants some peaches, Emily wants some new handcuffs—how the heck am I going to find 'official police handcuffs'? Steffy wants some hot dogs and the new Hooverphonic cd, Cinder wants some clove cigarettes and," she paused, incredulous, "a DVD of The Three Stooges. You gotta be kidding me. No wonder the generators keep running out of fuel…Steffy and Cinder are hooking up goodness knows how many devices to 'em."

Sid only chuckled and buckled up his knee-high oxblood boots.

"Where was I? Hmm…Desondra wants chocolate, Agate wants—oh lord—fuck-me-pumps!" Cady laughed over that last request on the list. She looked up at Sid whose Shikar-yellow eyes were wide with avid curiosity over such a request. "She actually wrote 'fuck-me-pumps' on here. The woman never ceases to surprise me."

About the author:

Sherri L. King lives in the American Mid-West with her husband, artist and illustrator Darrell King. Critically acclaimed author of The Horde Wars and Moon Lust series, her primary interests lie in the world of action packed paranormals, though she's been known to dabble in several other genres as time permits.

Sherri welcomes mail from readers. You can write to her c/o Ellora's Cave Publishing at 1337 Commerce Drive, Suite 13, Stow OH 44224.

Also by Sherri L. King:

Available in ebook

Moon Lust *Moon Lust*

Rayven's Awakening *Chronicles of the Aware*

Ravenous *The Horde Wars I*

Icarus —*Midnight Desires anthology*

Bitten *Moon Lust II*

Mating Season *Moon Lust III*

Wanton Fire *The Horde Wars II*

Bachelorette

Razor's Edge *The Horde Wars III*

Fetish

Feral Heat *Moon Lust IV*

Manaconda —Sacred Eden *The Horde Wars IV*

Lord Of The Deep *The Horde Wars V*

The Jewel

Overexposed *Voyeurs I — Ellora's Cavemen Tales from the Temple II anthology*

Available in Print

Primal Heat —Moon Lust *Moon Lust I*

Ravenous *The Horde Wars I*

Fetish

Manaconda —Sacred Eden *The Horde Wars IV*

Overexposed *Voyeurs I — Ellora's Cavemen Tales from the Temple II anthology*

Why an electronic book?

We live in the Information Age—an exciting time in the history of human civilization in which technology rules supreme and continues to progress in leaps and bounds every minute of every hour of every day. For a multitude of reasons, more and more avid literary fans are opting to purchase e-books instead of paperbacks. The question to those not yet initiated to the world of electronic reading is simply: *why?*

1. *Price.* An electronic title at Ellora's Cave Publishing runs anywhere from 40-75% less than the cover price of the <u>exact same title</u> in paperback format. Why? Cold mathematics. It is less expensive to publish an e-book than it is to publish a paperback, so the savings are passed along to the consumer.

2. *Space.* Running out of room to house your paperback books? That is one worry you will never have with electronic novels. For a low one-time cost, you can purchase a handheld computer designed specifically for e-reading purposes. Many e-readers are larger than the average handheld, giving you plenty of screen room. Better yet, hundreds of titles can be stored within your new library—a single microchip. (Please note that Ellora's Cave does not endorse any specific brands. You can check our website at www.ellorascave.com for customer recommendations we make available to new consumers.)

3. *Mobility.* Because your new library now consists of only a microchip, your entire cache of books can be taken with you wherever you go.

4. *Personal preferences are accounted for.* Are the words you are currently reading too small? Too large? Too...**ANNOYING**? Paperback books cannot be modified according to personal preferences, but e-books can.

5. *Innovation.* The way you read a book is not the only advancement the Information Age has gifted the literary community with. There is also the factor of what you can read. Ellora's Cave Publishing will be introducing a new line of interactive titles that are available in e-book format only.

6. *Instant gratification.* Is it the middle of the night and all the bookstores are closed? Are you tired of waiting days—sometimes weeks—for online and offline bookstores to ship the novels you bought? Ellora's Cave Publishing sells instantaneous downloads 24 hours a day, 7 days a week, 365 days a year. Our e-book delivery system is 100% automated, meaning your order is filled as soon as you pay for it.

Those are a few of the top reasons why electronic novels are displacing paperbacks for many an avid reader. As always, Ellora's Cave Publishing welcomes your questions and comments. We invite you to email us at service@ellorascave.com or write to us directly at: 1337 Commerce Drive, Suite 13, Stow OH 44224.

Discover for yourself why readers can't get enough of the multiple award-winning publisher Ellora's Cave. Whether you prefer e-books or paperbacks, be sure to visit EC on the web at www.ellorascave.com for an erotic reading experience that will leave you breathless.

WWW.ELLORASCAVE.COM

Printed in the United States
27256LVS00008B/1-72